Edward And The Christmas Grumps

Written and illustrated by

CHRISSIE DAINES

First Edition

ISBN: 978-1-791-72245-6
ISBN-13:

ACKNOWLEDGMENTS

With thanks to Jay and Connor, who's imagination helped craft this tale and to Michael for his role as editor.

To Tony,

Some pre-Christmas spice,

love

Chrissie

x

"It's All Perfectly Wonderful"

Aphrodite

MEET ARCHIE

When children dream of Christmas, it's usually about the wonderful things like Santa, his elves and Rudolph, but for some children their dream of Christmas can turn surprisingly grumpy.

This is just what happened to Edward and his big sister, Jill. When their Christmas dream began they were lost and alone in a dark mysterious wood on a cold winter's evening.

Luckily, the moon helped light their way as they followed winding paths lined by tall spindly pine trees and weird little bushes. Stumpy arrowed wooden signs of 'This Way' and 'That Way' were there to guide them, but only led them in circles.

"Where are we?" asked Edward, looking about nervously.

"We're lost," replied Jill.

"I know that, but *why* are we lost... and how did we get here?"

"Oh really Edward, if I knew that then we wouldn't be lost now, would we?" snapped Jill in frustration.

Edward had chocolate brown eyes and dark wavy hair hidden under a green woolly hat. He was a little short and thin for a boy of eight, though his scruffy coat disguised that perfectly. Curiously, for someone of that age, he was carrying a teddy bear with a torn ear.

Jill was two years older than her brother and quite a bit taller. She had brown eyes too, but her face was rounder with a sprinkle of freckles. Her mother had told her that the freckles were caused by a cheeky elf who flicked paint at her face while she slept on Christmas Eve. Jill believed it once, but no longer. Like Edward, Jill's hair was also dark, but straight with a fringe and reached her shoulders. She wore a bobble hat and jacket that was a golden colour similar to Edward's teddy.

Jill was getting worried, "Now come on, we have to keep going," she said.

"But I'm getting tired," muttered Edward, while dragging his feet.

"I can tell. I'm doing my best to get us out of here," replied Jill.

"And now my tummy's rumbling. Do we have any shortbread left?" he asked.

Jill was losing her patience, "No, my pockets are empty... and stop being a grump. I can't magic salvation from thin air, can I?"

Edward shook his head furiously and said, "I'm *not* being a grump and stop using big words. I don't like it and I don't like being lost... and Teddy doesn't either. He's scared."

"Nonsense, Teddy's a very brave bear. And salvation isn't a big word. It means *rescue* Edward. Now let's keep to this path. The sign said 'This Way' and look there's a bright light up ahead. It has to lead somewhere," said Jill.

"But the light's in the tree tops. I'm not climbing any trees, not in the dark," he said, anxiously scratching his chin.

"But, but, but Edward. It's always *but* with you," she replied, shaking her head. "And no, they'll be no tree climbing Edward. We'll be home by morning, you'll see."

Edward secretly whispered to his teddy, "Don't worry, we'll be home by morning."

They followed the light and came across a sign that read, 'Cottage Ahead'. Jill's mood perked up. "Look there's the cottage with a light on and smoke coming out of the chimney. We'll go there," she said, and began to walk faster.

"But that's not our house and smoke means there's a fire," Edward replied, doing his best to keep up, "And I don't like fire."

Jill tapped the back of her brother's head. "Don't be ridiculous Edward. It's all there is, now come on," she said firmly.

The house was a delightful little cottage crafted from logs of wood harvested from nearby trees. It had a small front garden with a simple white picket fence. The front gate was open. They walked through it and up a paved grey path lined with pretty white snowdrops. The path led to a crooked sparkly number six hung on a shiny red door with a big bizarre sign that read, 'Knock Here Quietly'.

"Stand behind me. I'll do the talking," Jill demanded.

So, when Jill knocked *'unquietly'*, Edward hid behind his sister. A clock chimed within the cottage. The children fidgeted as they waited. Eventually, the door opened. A slinky black cat appeared next to a pair of feet wearing gigantic reindeer-faced slippers. The door opened wider.

The children were greeted by a very tall woman in a red dressing gown with a white fur collar and cuffs. The letter A was embroidered in gold on each of its three pockets. She had big rollers in her mousy brown hair and a gloopy green beauty mask on her face.

The woman spoke in a surprisingly squeaky voice, “Ah children, you’ve arrived. How wonderful. We’ve been expecting you.” She took a second glance, “There are two of you, aren’t there?”

Edward bravely popped his head out from behind his sister’s back. The woman saw him, “Ah, there you are.”

Jill was puzzled, “I’m sorry but we’re very lost and this is the only...” she said, before being rudely interrupted.

“Oh there’s no need to explain, really. Come in out of the cold. There are two mugs of hot chocolate and some scrumptious shortbread biscuits waiting,” said the woman, cheerfully.

The children hesitated, so the woman encouraged them inside. “They’re your favourite. We just baked them especially for you,” she said and smiled widely, causing her beauty mask to make a strange squishy sound. The children couldn’t help but snigger.

Jill was very tempted by the offer, "We do love shortbread and we are so very hungry, aren't we Edward?"

He nodded eagerly, rubbing his hungry tummy.

"Fabulous. That's settled. In you come," said the woman. She immediately popped her head out of the door and looked around, "Quickly now, before the Christmas grumps grab you." She leered down at Edward, blinked hard twice and said, "Does the boy speak or has Kat got his tongue?"

Neither child answered. The cat seemed unimpressed. It meowed, turned up its nose, and wandered back into the cottage. They watched it settle by a log fire. Edward was highly amused by the woman's beauty mask and rollers. He whispered something in his sister's ear. They giggled as they went inside, much to the woman's delight, "Whispering, sneaky! Giggling, cheeky!" she said cheerfully.

The woman closed the front door, taking extra care to lock it. They stood in a small hall with garish pink and grey stripy wallpaper which led to a lounge painted in pale mustard yellow. As she walked, the woman had to duck sometimes to avoid banging her head on low wooden beams. Apart from the log fire, the lounge was lit by several scented candles. An old, out of time, clock ticked now and again above the fireplace. There was a worn out floral sofa and two matching wingback armchairs, a few small tables, shelves where more candles sat and two large framed paintings of a robin and the black cat. A faded patchwork rug lay in front of the fireplace. Beside the rug was an unusual painted wooden Christmas tree. There were no other decorations.

"Children, shall I take your hats and coats?" the woman asked.

Jill politely refused, "No thank you. We won't be staying long. We just need..." But once again she was interrupted. "Oh dear sweet Jill, you're both hungry and thirsty and in need of forty winks," said the woman. She gestured to the sofa, "Here, please sit." The children did so.

Two mugs of delicious smelling hot chocolate and a plate of shortbread were on a table right in front of them. Edward put his teddy on his lap and hugged it tightly. He stared uneasily at the log fire. He didn't much like it.

Jill was bemused. "How did you know my name? I didn't tell you that," she said frowning.

The woman sat heavily in her armchair. Boing! A spring popped. "Did you not?" she replied, then leant forward and looked under the chair. A broken spring was poking out. "Maybe it was just a good guess," she mumbled as a bit of her beauty mask dripped from her nose on to the rug. Plop! She straightened up and rubbed it in with her slipper, smiling widely and making her mask squelch.

Surprised, the children screwed up their faces. The amused woman copied them. She scrunched up her face, causing the squidgy noise again. "Oh, I must apologise for my appearance children. You were a little early and I'm getting ready for my big day! It won't be long now," she said, rubbing her hands together.

Jill smiled and took a sip of the best hot chocolate she'd ever tasted, while Edward tucked into the amazing shortbread. The cat just sat and stared at them through squinting golden eyes.

"Your beds are made," said the woman. "There are two pairs of jim-jams neatly folded, dressing gowns and slippers. I won't be lighting the fire anymore, but you'll find plenty of Christmas jumpers to keep you warm."

Bemused, the children looked at each other, unsure what to do. The woman added, "Oh, and to turn the candles on, just click your fingers once. It's twice for off." She did just that. The children gasped when they saw the candles turn on and off by themselves. Edward desperately tried to click his fingers but couldn't manage it. "Oh fiddlesticks," he whispered ever so quietly. Oddly, a small flame on a candle didn't trouble him like the log fire did. Jill said nothing about the candles. She was too busy thinking.

The woman spoke again, "Oh, and my toothbrush is sparkly red. Yours are gold and green. It's important we look after our teeth."

Wary of strangers, Jill was unsure what to do. "It's terribly kind of you but we can't possibly stay here," she said, clicking her fingers twice. They were all in the dark, apart from the firelight. She gave in to her curiosity and asked, "How do the candles do that?"

"You'll find out soon enough," said the woman.

Jill was troubled by that answer. "Oh, do you have a phone? I'd like to ring my mother," she asked.

"No, we don't have a phone," said the woman quickly, before clicking her fingers again to relight the candles. Edward smiled. He was beginning to like it at the cottage.

"A laptop or tablet?" asked Jill.

"No. Sorry," said the woman, adding slowly, "The cottage has *no* electricity."

"No electricity?" replied Jill with a gulp. "Could we possibly speak to your neighbours? They can't be far as your cottage has number six on the door."

"We don't have any *real* neighbours. And there's a good reason why this cottage is number six. May I suggest we worry about all this in the morning? You've been wandering about lost for far too long to remember."

"But I *do* remember the odd sign on your door, 'Knock Here Quietly'?"

"It's not odd, it's essential. Unexpected loud noises can scare young fairies and attract the Christmas grumps," she said, taking a mouthful of shortbread.

Jill was grinning. "The Christmas grumps? That's ridiculous and there's no such thing as fairies," she said firmly.

The woman mumbled a reply with a mouthful of biscuit, "Better safe than sorry. Now tell me, does the teddy have a name?"

"He's just called Teddy. He's extremely special. It was a present from Santa for Edward's First Christmas."

The woman crossed her legs and tapped her nose, "Hmm. Eddie's teddy... a teddy for Edward, Ted and Ed, Ed's Ted, Tedward for short." She took another mouthful of biscuit.

Edward finally spoke, "But Daddy says I'm too old for Teddy. He says I need to grow up fast."

Taken completely by surprise, the woman jumped up and spluttered crumbs all over the rug. Some landed on the cat, causing it to leap into the air. Jill giggled.

The woman came over to Edward, "I'm sorry child! I was sure Kat had your tongue." She looked at her cat and it flapped its ears. She continued, "Teddy is very welcome here. Oh, look at his ear, it's all unstitched. We'll have to put that right."

Jill spoke for her brother, "That's kind of you. Err... I'm sorry but you didn't tell us *your* name."

"Did I not? You can call me Aphrodite!" She gave a little twirl, almost stumbling because of her giant slippers and only just avoided banging her head on a wooden beam.

"Aphrodite, the Greek goddess of beauty?" said Jill giggling.

"Yes! *Obviously!*" said Aphrodite firmly, adding, "You've already met Kat. Now it's time to meet Archie."

She pointed enthusiastically at the wooden Christmas tree. It was about three feet tall with a star on top and numbers painted on doors with small handles.

"Archie, where?" asked Jill.

"Here, my Christmas tree. May I present Archie the Advent calendar? Take good care of Archie. He's very special. It's the first of December tomorrow." She rubbed her hands together gleefully. "And you have been invited as our special guests to open door number one in the morning."

In celebration, Kat raised a paw at the children, but Edward wasn't at all impressed. "But I *don't* like Christmas," he said coldly.

"Edward, how can you say such a thing? You always loved Christmas."

"Not anymore. I don't like Christmas, not one bit."

Startled, Aphrodite blurted out, "Oooohh, the Grump Grumble! We don't want that, especially not in this house. It's why you're here Edward. Let's see if Archie can fill your heart with love for Christmas again, shall we?"

Edward shook his head, "No. It won't happen. Some things are just impossible." He put Teddy to one side, stood, and removed his hat and coat. He was wearing scuffed trainers, jeans and a T-shirt with a picture of a fist-punching, green-skinned man. Aphrodite didn't much like the strange green man. She said nothing about it as she sat down again, but very gently this time.

"Okay. I've decided we'll stay. But just for tonight," said Jill. She took off her hat and used her fingers to tidy her fringe.

"Oh goody, goody gumdrops," cried Aphrodite, clapping her hands. She shook her head in excitement. Her hair rollers wobbled and some of her beauty mask splashed over her armchair. A green dollop landed on the clock with a plop and sprinkled the cat.

"Oh look, Kat has got the cream!"

The children giggled.

***

Aphrodite showed the children to their bedrooms, but didn't dare enter because they both had 'No Grown-Ups Allowed' signs on the doors. The children took a look around. Each room had a creaking old bed with a thin mattress, a small wardrobe, a chest of drawers packed with Christmas jumpers and curtains with robin patterns. Alarmingly, the rooms had no heating, just hot water bottles.

"Hot water bottles!" gasped Edward.

"Wonderful, isn't it? Things are warming up very nicely," replied Aphrodite from the corridor.

The only games the children could find were chess, draughts, and snakes and ladders. There was also a pack of playing cards, colouring pencils and paper and a handful of bedtime story books.

"There are no toys!" said Jill.

"Isn't it stupendous? We'll make our own entertainment," replied Aphrodite, and left the children alone for a while to settle in.

When she returned, she found Edward stood on a low wobbly stool leaning over a tiny basin in a pokey bathroom holding the green toothbrush.

"You chose the green one," Aphrodite said.

"Green's my favourite colour," he replied, yawning.

"Yes, I guessed as much," she said, then waited for Edward to return to his room. When the children were comfortable in their beds, she cried, "Good night children. Let's hope it's not a grumpy one." She double-clicked her fingers to turn off scented candles labelled, 'Sweet Dreams', but poor Edward couldn't sleep at all, not one wink. Even cuddling Teddy made no difference.

***

In the morning the cottage was eerily quiet. When the children got up they left their beds unmade and put on their dressing gowns and slippers. Kat was waiting for them at the top of the stairs. She followed them down, listening as the children continued to complain about the cottage.

"Sheets and blankets, and a lumpy pillow? That won't do at all!" said Jill.

"And the games are awful! What shall we do all day? We can't just draw and colour in."

Kat flapped her ears.

"Well, it doesn't really matter because once we've had breakfast, we're leaving," said Jill.

"Shush," Edward whispered, "Aphrodite might hear you."

"I very much doubt that's her real name. And I'll do the shushing if you don't mind. Besides I think she's gone out."

Edward doubted that, "We're just children. Do you really think she'd leave us alone in her house?"

"Yes Edward, I do. But it's fine. I'll look after you. I always do."

Jill was right. They were totally alone in the cottage, apart from Kat. They went in search of breakfast and found a small kitchen. It had a few pale blue cupboards with some handles missing, a tiny sink with an annoying dripping tap, a scruffy old fridge and a wood burning cooker. There was a wonky wooden table and three worn out chairs.

They were pleasantly surprised to find the table laid for breakfast. There was toast, orange juice, porridge, fruit and cereal, all served on a jumble of different plates, bowls and cutlery. Edward sat Teddy on one of the chairs and they happily tucked in. It was all extremely tasty but afterwards they didn't think to wash the dishes or clear the table. In fact, they left Kat licking at the butter dish.

"I wonder where Aphrodite could be?" asked Edward.
"Polishing her broomstick, I'd guess."
"Well if she's a witch, why did she make us such a lovely breakfast?"

Jill was convinced of it. She blurted out, "Because it's a trick! She knew we were coming didn't she? She knew my name! She knew we loved shortbread and she lights candles by clicking her fingers. She also has a black cat. Let's get dressed and leave, while we still can."

Edward simply shrugged his shoulders and sighed, mumbling, "Okay."

They went into the lounge. Jill noticed their coats and hats were hung up by the front door, above Aphrodite's reindeer slippers.

"I wish I could click my fingers. It's very annoying," said Edward.

"And *so* are you!" replied Jill.

"No I'm not! I like the magic candles and I don't think Aphrodite's a witch. Anyway, if we leave where will we go?"

Kat meowed to get their attention. She rubbed up against the Advent calendar, purring loudly.

Edward noticed her, "Look, door number one, I think Kat wants you to open it and Aphrodite said we should."

"Let's ignore her. It's probably another trick! Anyway, yesterday you said you hated Christmas!"

"No I didn't."

"Oh yes you did."

"Oh no I didn't."

"Oh yes you did."

"I didn't. I said 'I don't like it!'"

Jill wagged her finger furiously at her brother, "Fine! Maybe Aphrodite was right, you're getting the grumps."

"I'm happy being a grump," said Edward defiantly.

***

Putting on their coats and hats they headed for the front door, which was unlocked. Once outside they remembered that the cottage was surrounded by woods and those mesmerising meandering paths with arrowed signposts reading, 'This Way' or 'That Way' and 'Try Here' or 'Try There'. Once again, the children did as they suggested, but once again every path led to the sign, 'Cottage Ahead' and took them back to the start.

Jill wasn't ready to give up easily. "If she got out, so can we!" she said.

"Maybe she left us alone because today is her big day."

"Edward can you please be quiet. I'm trying to remember which way we've been."

"Going round in circles, that's where. Now I'm really tired and my arm hurts from carrying Teddy. Can we go back, please?" he urged.

"No. Not yet. I'm in charge, remember? Here, give me Ted! I'll hold him for you," she said firmly as she snatched hold of the bear.

"But I didn't get my forty winks last night."

"'Forty winks', that's just what she said! Why do you keep talking about her? You actually *like* her, don't you?"

Edward was getting tearful, "Stop picking on me."

"I'm not picking on you Edward. I'm just cross with you." She wagged her finger at Edward again, more furiously than ever.

"Why did you tell her first that you hate Christmas? I'm your sister, you should have told me."

"I didn't get the chance. Anyway, I can't tell you why I *don't* like Christmas. You're not ready yet," he said walking away.

"Nonsense! What do you mean, I'm not ready? I'm much bigger than you are Edward! Now I'm really cross. I'm done with this. I'm going back to the cottage."

Jill deliberately dropped the teddy and stomped off. A bold robin landed on Teddy then quickly flew away again, perhaps because of the cat that had been secretly following them all. It rubbed against Teddy, purring. Edward stroked Kat.

"I'm sorry Teddy. I never said I liked her, did I?" whispered Edward, "But I don't think she's a witch."

Suddenly, Edward heard a strange shuffling noise in the woods. For a moment he thought he saw a pair of glowing orange eyes looking back at him from amongst some bushes.

Startled, Edward quickly grabbed his teddy and found the energy to race with Kat back to the cottage. He called to his sister, "Jill, I'm really sorry. Wait for me!"

When they reached the cottage, Jill deliberately disobeyed the 'Knock Here Quietly' sign. Instead, she knocked loudly. There was no answer. She tried the handle and the door was still unlocked. Edward caught her up and they went inside.

"You knocked loudly. You're not supposed to do that because of the fairies," he said, catching his breath.

"Fairies aren't real Edward and if they were, do you think for one minute they'd choose to live in a horrid little cottage in the middle of nowhere?"

"I was just saying because it says so on the sign."

"Mmm," she replied, then called, "Hello Aphrodite. It's us. Eh... we've been for a little walk in the woods."

But there was no reply.

"That's a fib. We were trying to escape. You always told me to tell the truth."

Jill whispered, "Shush. She might hear you. Anyway, it's not a lie. I'm just pretending that's all. There's a difference."

"So it's alright to pretend then, is it?"

Jill cupped a hand to an ear, and said, "Be quiet Edward. I'm listening out for her."

But they heard nothing other than the cat flapping her ears. They took off their coats and hung them back up on the pegs by the door. They were still dressed in yesterday's clothes.

Jill wore a purple jumper, jeans and matching purple boots. They went into the kitchen and were astonished to find all the breakfast dishes put away. They had been replaced by plates of sandwiches, crisps and warm, freshly baked, brownies. There was a bowl of food on the floor for Kat.

"Now she's made us lunch. See, I told you she's *not* a witch," said Edward smugly.

"She must have come in and gone back out again."

The children ate their lunch then settled on the sofa. The splashed beauty cream mask and biscuit crumbs from the day before had been cleared away. Kat pawed eagerly at the Advent calendar.

"Do you think Aphrodite will come back soon?" Edward asked.

"See, you do like her, don't you? That's why you said she's not a witch, isn't it!" said Jill stiffly.

"I never said that! Stop picking on me," replied Edward. He got up and moved to one of the armchairs.

"Now you've got the hump."

"I'm happy having the hump."

Jill looked at her brother harshly, "Tell me why you don't like Christmas, Edward?"

He shook his head, "No. I would if I could, but I can't. I've already told you, you're not ready."

"That's ridiculous. Right! Like it or not, I'm going to open the first door on Archie the Advent Calendar and I'm going to do it on my own." She went over to the wooden tree and added, "Let's see what you make of that then, shall we?"

"Fine! Do it! I don't care. I didn't want to watch you anyway," said Edward tearfully.

"Grumpy, humpy, don't like Christmas," teased Jill. She poked out her tongue.

Edward stood up and said, "I'm happy being a grump. I'm happy having the hump. I don't like Christmas, not one bit!"

He stormed off upstairs with Teddy. Kat followed him.

DOOR ONE

Jill knelt before the Advent calendar. As she closed her eyes and gently pulled on door one she had a wild thought, 'This could be the best Christmas ever!' The calendar door opened and she looked inside. She was really excited to discover a small box with clowns painted on it. On the back of the door was an identical picture of a jack-in-the-box. She reached in, took the box out and studied it. There were paintings of juggling clowns on all four sides and a tiny turning crank handle. Curious, she tipped the box upside down and was surprised to find her name scrawled in gold ink on the base.

"How ridiculous, this can't possibly be mine. It's much too small anyway!" she said, talking to herself.

She turned the box the right way up and put it on the rug. Suddenly, with a sparkle and flash it got much bigger.

"Extraordinary," she cried, "Maybe you really are mine!"

Carefully, she turned the handle on the jack-in-the-box. It played the familiar tune 'Pop Goes the Weasel'. On the word 'pop', the lid sprang open, but Jack didn't pop out.

Jill sighed, "Ah, I remember now. Your spring was broken."

She reached inside to try to pull out the jack.

"I say. Steady on there. You're hurting me," squealed Jack, as she pulled the jack free.

Jill shrieked and backed away. She watched in utter amazement as Jack wriggled the rest of the way out of the box and stretched out his arms. Jack was wearing a blue and yellow Harlequin suit and hat. He was a jester with a beaming face and smiling eyes.

"Ah, freedom! I must say I'd forgotten what this felt like," he said joyfully.

"You can talk?" uttered Jill in disbelief.

"Well observed Jill. That's a promising start," said Jack in a pompous and elegant voice. Every word was said precisely and accurately.

"This is crazy," claimed Jill.

"Isn't it just? This is where you say, 'Wake me up, I must be dreaming!'" said Jack ironically.

"Yes, that's it!" She pinched her arm and said, "I must be dreaming. It explains absolutely everything."

"Splendid. Now we have the incredulity... or shall I say disbelief... out of the way, shall we continue? Aphrodite could return any second and her enthusiasm is infuriatingly tiresome."

"'Infuriatingly tiresome'? I like those words."

"Yes. In my condition, I can't much be doing with any of that. I'm kept in this dark box for months on end and when I finally pop up my spring's broken. The last thing I need is to be told that everything's perfectly wonderful."

"You really are in a terrible muddle. I'm sorry about your spring Jack, but *I'm* here now."

"You are and there's much to say and do. Oh Jill, I remember when you were younger, you used to ask me about all of lives great mysteries. A particular favourite of mine was why Jack and Jill fell down the hill fetching a pail of water."

"Jack and Jill, ha, you broke your crown and I came tumbling after!"

"I always liked that bit. Now listen, I'm not the only gift. There are twenty four of us to be precise and you can't play at this game without imagination, so I'm glad you still have yours."

"Play?" asked Jill.

"Yes, play. Shall we begin? There are things I need to tell you. It's important to listen very carefully."

"Listen carefully?"

"Yes, I need to tell you the rules to Archie's Advent Adventure."

"Rules?"

"Yes rules! I call them Santa's clauses," said Jack with a laugh.

"Santa's clauses? That's confusing. It sounds like Santa Claus?" suggested Jill, scratching her head.

"Well, maybe he's called Santa Claus because of the clauses in this game. Clause is another word for a rule."

"Clause is another word for a rule?"

"Yes! No more interruptions, please. My memory isn't what it once was and I don't want to get anything wrong. Listen carefully. Now, rule one: Archie's calendar doors must only be opened sequentially… that means in the right order. Rule two: Once you've opened the first door, which you just did, you can only succeed in this game by opening all the other doors on the correct day. For example, door two must be opened on December the second."

"Sequentially and on the right date?" she replied, "Hang on. We can't stay here for twenty-five days. That's ridiculous!"

"It's not ridiculous at all. When children dream of Christmas the dream can sometimes seem to last for years and years, but when the dream ends it's as though only one night has passed. It's a very special night, Christmas Eve in fact."

"So it is a dream and I'm having the dream on Christmas Eve?" said Jill with a twinkle in her eye. She rubbed her hands together in excitement.

"Please no more interruptions, I'm concentrating. It's essential I get this right, Christmas depends upon it."

"Christmas depends upon it?" she replied.

"Will you please stop copying me? You're not a parrot. Now, rule three: You must use Archie's daily gifts wisely and do not lose any of the pieces. Oh, and if any are broken or damaged in some way, you mustn't try to fix them."

"That sounds like three rules rolled into one."

"It is. You're listening, excellent! Rule four: You must not under any circumstances eat anything that Archie gives you. Absolutely not! Rule six."

"No, rule five?"

"Oh exactly, yes. I apologise. I did say I was forgetful, didn't I? Did I?"

"I can't remember," replied Jill.

"Well I am." Jack continued, "Now, rule five: Once the adventure has begun, and up until Christmas Day, you or any other players must never, ever, say the words, 'I don't believe in Father Christmas'. Is that perfectly clear?"

"Perfectly clear."

"Rule six. Yes, I'm sure there's a rule six. It'll come to me. There's more, I know it. Now what was it?" Jack tapped on his box for a few seconds. "No, sorry it's gone. I'll come back to it. It's my wonky spring. It makes me a little forgetful."

"Don't worry about it Jack. Just tell me when you remember."

"I will. Provided I remember to tell you that I've remembered what it was I forgot." He tapped his box again, "I think that's right, is it?"

"Yes Jack. So, if I fail in Archie's Advent Adventure what happens to Christmas?" asked Jill, worried by the responsibility.

"It's all, me, myself and I with you, isn't it? Your brother is part of this adventure too. He just doesn't know it yet. As for what happens if you fail in this game... Christmas will be cancelled!"

"Cancelled?" asked Jill, shocked.

"No Santa. No presents for any child, good, bad or otherwise! Not just this year... but every year... *forever!*"

"*Forever?* I'm sorry but that's simply ridiculous. I cannot possibly allow that to happen. Wait here... I'll get Edward."

"Wait here she says! As if I can go anywhere?" mumbled Jack.

Jill dashed upstairs, almost falling over Kat who was sat on the middle step.

"Edward, come quickly. I've something incredible to show you," she urged.

Edward was already on his way slowly down the stairs, with Teddy in hand.

"What?" he asked, sulkily.

Jill grabbed her brother's free hand and made him hurry. Kat followed.
"But we're not supposed to run down stairs, remember?"

When they reached the lounge, Jill pointed excitedly at the jack-in-the-box.
"Hello Edward, remember me? We need to talk. I trust you are well?" asked Jack.
But Edward said nothing.
"Well?" asked Jill.
"Well, what?" said Edward. He crossed his arms.
"Are you well? He asked if you are well. Come now Edward, don't be rude, answer him."
Edward shook his head, "Who asked me?"
"Why, he did," insisted Jill. She led Edward closer to Jack and pointed right at him.

"Are you lying again? It's just a toy. Toy's can't talk, everyone knows that."

Jack had an idea what had happened to Edward, "Its bad news I'm afraid. He's lost his imagination. It appears Edward can't see or hear the *real* me!"

Jill didn't believe it, "I'm not lying or pretending. Look closer Edward, it's my old jack-in-the-box. Don't you remember it? I was given Jack on my first Christmas. It's definitely him. He's spring is still broken. Edward, Jack just spoke to me. He told me Christmas would be cancelled forever and ever unless we win at Archie's Advent Adventure. He explained all the rules of the game. We have no choice now. We have to try to save Christmas!"

"A broken spring?" said Edward casually, "But I told you already. I don't like Christmas."

"Edward, why do you keep saying that?"

"Because *I don't believe in Father Christmas* anymore!" he snapped.

Jack was dismayed, "No. It's a nightmare. I fear your brother has caught the Christmas grumps." Horrified, the jack-in-the-box panicked and pulled down his lid.

As he did so, the cottage front door flew open. It was Aphrodite. She stomped inside wearing a long matted shaggy brown coat, heavy clumpy laced-up boots and stylishly cool sunglasses. She had crazily wild hair full of large stuck up curls.

"Children, I'm back! Did you miss me? It's perfectly wonderful to be..." she said.

But Jill interrupted her, "Aphrodite, am I really glad to see you? We've only just started Archie's Advent Adventure and Edward has already said, '*I don't believe in Father Christmas*'."

"Oh dear, and you just said it again! It's marvellous mayhem."

"Jack told me that if we said *it* then Christmas would be lost forever." said Jill uneasily.

"Did he now? That's the trouble with Jack. Because of his spring he doesn't get everything exactly right. You've still got one more chance. This game's like baseball... three strikes and you're out!"

"Phew!" said Jill relieved, "But Edward's lost his imagination too... he can't see or hear Jack."

"How perfect, it's just part of the game," replied Aphrodite.

She threw her coat over the jack-in-the-box, pulled her laces and kicked off her clumpy boots, tossed her sunglasses away and walked towards Archie. She failed to duck, so the stuck up curls at the top of her head scraped along a wooden beam. Some of the curls snapped off and stuck fast. "Whoops. I fear I put on far too much hairspray. It made my wonderful curls as sticky and hard as nails dipped in glue," said Aphrodite, as she admired her dangling curls stuck on the beam. "Still it's just as I had hoped. They'll make perfect little perches."

Aphrodite smiled at the children, unaware that the twisted curls left on her head looked like reindeer antlers.

She slumped heavily into her wing-backed armchair. Boing! Another spring had popped out. She bent her head forward to check under the chair and accidentally poked the patchwork rug with her stiff 'antler' like hair.

"Oh fiddlesticks!" she mumbled.

The children giggled. It was becoming a habit

DOOR TWO

In the morning the children were again alone in the cottage. They got up, put on their dressing gowns and slippers and headed straight for the kitchen. Kat was waiting patiently and followed them down the stairs, weaving in and out of their feet. Another splendid breakfast had been prepared, including cereal, pancakes and waffles, but Jill had lost her appetite. She merely picked at her food, preferring instead to watch Kat drink milk from her bowl.

"At least my pillow wasn't so lumpy last night. I think someone changed it," she said, glumly.

"Mine wasn't lumpy either, not that it helped much," replied Edward, trying over and over to click his fingers, but failing miserably. Jill was so glum she didn't even bother to tell him to stop.

Edward knew something wasn't right with his sister, "Are you sad because of me? I'm sorry for what I said about you know who, but you said it too and Aphrodite said we still have one more chance left."

"It's not that Edward. I'm upset because I've been way too mean to you and now you've lost your imagination... or worse I was imagining the whole thing and Jack isn't real, and I don't want to think about that."

"Then don't," replied Edward. "Aphrodite believed you, didn't she? And I could try to get my imagination back. Remember I talk to Teddy sometimes, don't I? I could always just pretend to see Jack if you like," he said with a gaping yawn.

"I suppose so, Edward," she said, looking properly at her brother for the first time that morning. "Oh, Edward, your eyes... what have you done? You have terrible dark circles under them."

"Not sleeping, that's what. Not one wink for two nights," he said. "I don't know what I'd do without all this yummy food... have you tried the waffles, Teddy loves them."

Jill had a thought, "Perhaps some children just can't sleep in their dreams, and you just happen to be one of them." Her appetite was slowly returning. She took a mouthful of waffle.

"In my dreams? What are you talking about? He asked whilst chewing.

"Well Jack says it is... and on Christmas Eve too."

Edward swallowed, licked his lips then screwed up his nose. "This food tastes way too good for a dream," he claimed.

"Well it makes sense to me. Got any better ideas?"

"Yes, I have actually. Jill, I was wondering, when are you going to open door two? Can I watch you this time? I'd like Teddy to see it too."

Jill smiled widely. "Let's do it now Edward!" she said, and leapt off the chair, knocking it sideways and alarming Kat, who hissed and spat at it.

"Yes, let's," agreed Edward.

He followed Jill into the lounge and sat beside her in front of the calendar. The jack-in-the-box was next to it on a small table. Jack was still in his box.

Edward put Teddy on his lap. "Look Teddy, Jill's going to open door two," he said, playing along with the game.

"No, why don't you do it? Jack told me you could play too."

"Did he? Alright, I will," replied Edward. He opened door number two.

Inside was a round sweet in a gold wrapper. Its picture was painted on the back of the door. Edward removed the sweet and showed it to his sister, Teddy and the cat.

"That's a bit disappointing. It's just a boring old penny sweet, like the ones Grandma has at Christmas," he said.

"Not quite, Edward. Look, there's a picture of Santa's head on each side," said Jill cheerily.

"Ooh, I could bite off his head?" said Edward cheekily, as he pointed menacingly at one of the heads.

"Edward!" shrieked Jill. "You really mustn't. Jack said, 'Under absolutely no circumstances are we to eat any of Archie's gifts'."

Kat had joined them and meowed loudly in agreement.

"Did he? Oh, well he's pretty quiet now, isn't he," he said, looking at Jack's closed box.

"Well. I've not wound him up yet," said Jill in his defence.

"Anyway, it's probably just a boiled sweet or a toffee, and I don't much like either. I'm going to finish my breakfast," said Edward, flicking the sweet in the air like a coin then catching it as it fell.

Kat watched it spin then flapped her ears. She followed Edward after he stood up and marched into the kitchen holding his teddy and the Santa Sweet.

Jill was toying with winding up Jack when she heard Edward cry, "That's impossible!" Flabbergasted, he ran back to the lounge, almost falling over the cat, busy following him about like he was a mouse. "Jill someone's cleared away the breakfast. The dishes are all washed up and everything!"

"Edward! Now who's telling fibs?"

"What? Do I look like I'm telling fibs?" he asked.

"No Edward, you don't."

It turned out Edward was being absolutely one hundred and ten percent truthful. Jill had a disturbing thought, "Edward, I think someone else is living here... let's take a look around," she said.

***

A search of the cottage began, starting with the ground floor. They looked in every room, in every cupboard, behind every curtain and under every chair, but found no one. Zilch! They bravely headed upstairs, with Kat getting tangled under their feet. When they entered the bedrooms, they were astounded to find their beds made.

"Oh! You're definitely right. There's got to be someone else in here," said Edward. They went to the bathroom. Edward quickly grabbed the loo brush and planned to use it to defend himself. Jill took hold of a long handle bath brush, and practised a swipe or two, just in case.

"Keep together, stay behind me," she said.

Edward nodded.

There was only one place left to search - Aphrodite's room, but it had a sign on the door that read, 'No Children Allowed!'

Jill wasn't afraid to break the rules. "Let's go in!" she whispered, carefully opening the door.

"But, the sign says we mustn't."

"Oh, come on Edward!"

The children bravely stepped into Aphrodite's bedroom. Kat was irked and scratched the door frame in protest.

The room was decorated in deep shades of red, gold and green.
"It's just like being inside a giant Christmas cracker," said Jill.
"Bang!" called Edward, pretending to be one, confident that there was no intruder here.

The crazy room stunk of hairspray and was messy and jam-packed with all kinds of oddities. There were bundles of beauty products piled high on a dressing table, including jars of the gloopy green face mask, hair removing cream, tweezers, toe-nail clippers and many brushes tangled in matted brown hair. A shelf overwhelmed with books bowed under the weight of titles like, 'Glamorous You', 'Find the Beauty Within' and 'Enormous is the New Tiny.' An old-fashioned instant camera dangled perilously on a strap at one end of the shelf.

Beneath the camera were other shelves with a huge collection of partly-used scented candles with labels like, Scottish Shortbread, Chocolate Brownies and Lemon Puffs. Some candles were considerably less appealing like, Smelly Wellie Feet and Soggy Sprout Farts. One labelled Gooey Ear Wax had dried drips about its rim. Yuk! And another was called, Fit of the Giggles, which was just what the children had.

Jill dared to open a wardrobe door, almost causing it to topple over. The wardrobe was crammed full with old fashioned crimpled long-sleeved blouses in shades of red, gold and green. Beneath them were piles of neatly folded Christmas themed trouser bottoms. Many pairs of large shoes of considerable bad taste were lined up against a wall. Jill tried on a few, and clowned around in them. She wobbled awkwardly about the room, using the bath brush to help steady herself.

Above the shoes was a chart headed My Big Day with a scrawled To-Do list that began, 'Curl hair', which had a tick against it. Other tasks listed were, 'file and paint nails', 'clean dirt from belly button', 'squeeze spot on end of nose' and so on. Edward pointed at them with the bristly end of the loo brush. Kat glared in disapproval and continued to claw at the door frame.

Suddenly, they heard the front door slam. It was Aphrodite. "Children, I'm home. All is calm, all is bright, which gives me more time to prepare for my big day... children! CHILDREN!" she cried joyfully.

Before you knew it, the children had dashed from her room, closing the door behind them. They were at the top of the stairs, still holding up the loo and bath brushes.

Jill called out, "We're upstairs... just been... erm cleaning."

Edward smirked and whispered, "You lied again! That's twice now."

Jill nudged her brother and whispered back, "Shush. I'm just pretending remember."

"So it is alright to pretend then," said Edward.

Aphrodite reached the bottom of the stairs. She was wearing her shaggy brown coat again and her hair looked more like reindeer antlers than ever, "That's very peculiar. I hope you didn't clear the breakfast things away too. The cottage takes good care of itself, you know. It cooks, cleans, polishes and scrubs, does the ironing... and the washing. Most stupendous, don't you think?"

As she spoke the children were slowly coming down the stairs. They had a bird's eye view of a glowing red spot emerging on the tip of Aphrodite's nose. She was tapping it with a finger.

"That's amazing," said Edward. He was very tempted to scratch it with the end of the loo brush.

"It's incredible," mumbled Jill.

"It is, isn't it?" agreed Aphrodite, gesturing to the children to put the brushes back.

The children giggled, and dashed back up to the bathroom. Kat didn't follow them this time. Instead she flapped her ears right at Aphrodite.

DOOR THREE

When Edward got up on December the Third the shadows under his eyes were worse than ever. He still hadn't slept, not one bit. He did his best to wake himself up. He even tried brushing his hair for the first time in forever, but it made no difference. Tired of wearing the same clothes, Jill put on one of the Christmas jumpers. It had a picture of a Christmas Tree on it, but Edward was too weary to care.

After breakfast, Edward put his feet up on the sofa with Teddy to watch Jill open door three. She gave it just the gentlest of tugs, yet it opened really swiftly. A little red robin flew out. As with the previous gifts, its picture was on the inside of the door. The robin darted rapidly about the room, chirping happily in celebration. It soon settled on one of Aphrodite's hooks of curly hair still stuck on the beam.

"It's a robin, just like the one that landed on Teddy in the woods," said Edward with a yawn.

The cat gawked at it.

"Ah, isn't it pretty, look it's perched on Aphrodite's hair," Jill replied, looking up.

The robin sang merrily. However, its chirping attracted others of its kind. The first robin landed on a ledge outside the window, and playfully pecked the pane. Another arrived, then another. Edward sat up, "Oh look, there are more of them." He yawned and stretched his arms.

Jill was thinking about turning Jack's handle to introduce him to Edward but was distracted by the birds. She skipped over to the window. She couldn't believe what she was seeing. Tens then hundreds of robins landed on the picket fencing and front lawn. They hopped about, picking up sticks and pecking at things. "Oh my goodness, how lovely. Let's go outside. We have to see this!" said Jill.

"But I'm sleepy and we've no coats on!"

"Oh come on Edward. There's no time for that, hurry up and wake up or you'll miss it."

Edward somehow found the energy to do as she asked. The front door was unlocked. They opened it and dashed outside still wearing their slippers. There were robins in the trees, on the rooftop, on the chimney, just everywhere.

"Oh look, one's landed on my shoulder," said Edward.

"And one's tugging at my hair... the cheeky little thing," said Jill, trying to get it to settle. Kat, sensing a meal, crouched, wriggled her bottom and readied to pounce.

Thankfully, a sudden sharp clap of hands sent all the robins fluttering skyward, except for two, the one perched on Edward's shoulder and the other toying with Jill's hair.

The clap of hands came from Aphrodite, returning home unexpectedly early in her sunglasses, shaggy coat and clumpy boots, "Ah, there you are children. Jill, I see you're wearing a Christmas jumper. How marvellous and the robins have arrived. You must have opened door three. Aren't they a-door-able? They fill my heart with joy. Such splendid creatures... kept busy catching all those happy memories. They're priceless. I had one of my own, but alas no more. Take good care of yours and don't be alarmed if they fly away now and again. They always return though, until they're called away for good. You're very welcome to name yours, should you wish. I called mine Robin."

"Robin the robin, just like Kat the cat?" said Edward.

"Not quite Edward. Kat is short for Katrina you see."

"Oh," said Edward. "I didn't think of that." He had an idea, "Let's call our Robin's Peter and Paul, can we please?"

Aphrodite loved the suggestion. "Fly away Peter, fly away Paul. Come back Peter, come back Paul," she sang with her arms spread as wide as branches on a tree. "It brings a joyful tear to my eye."

Aphrodite took off her sunglasses and approached the children. A plaster on her nose began to come unstuck and dangled, revealing an enormous shiny red spot. A third robin appeared, swooped down, skilfully snatched the plaster and made off with it.

"That's not something you see every day now, is it children?" said Aphrodite. They all chuckled. Edward whispered in Jill's ear, "Perhaps Aphrodite's real name is Rudolph?"

"Oh there we are, at it again! Whispering, sneaky! Giggling, cheeky! Just remember children," she added, "Kat hears everything, don't you Kat? And you can tell when she's listening because of her cat flap!"

Kat flapped her ears and curled her tail.

The children giggled once more.

DOOR FOUR

On December the Fourth, Jill was in another of her bossy moods. She decided that in most games players usually take turns, but in some games it's possible to win another turn or lose one, so, because Edward chose the robins names she had earned the right to take another turn at opening one of Archie's doors. Phew!

"But that's cheating," said Edward, wearily.

"No it isn't. Jack didn't say anything about taking turns."

"But it's not very fair, is it?"

"Fair? Well you chose both the robins' names didn't you? And you don't even like Christmas anyway."

"I'm too tired to argue with you," he said, scratching once more on an annoying itch on his chin. "I'd probably just get another silly sweet anyway."

Jill was wearing another of the Christmas jumpers. It had a robin on it this time, but Edward kept to his angry green man T-shirt. He sat crossed legged on the rug, busily scratching that itch. Peter and Paul were watching from the safety of the hooks of Aphrodite's hair.

Kat ignored them and watched Jill open door four. She wasn't disappointed. Out flew a dazzling Christmas fairy with long dark hair, wearing a sparkling red dress and matching ballerina shoes. The fairy fluttered about the room before landing gracefully on the clock.

Jill was absolutely thrilled, "Aphrodite *was* right. Fairies are real... and look she's a Christmas fairy. Wow! Isn't she beautiful?"

Edward snorted, "Fairies, yuk! Christmas fairies, double yuk! I'm glad I didn't open that door."

"Where did she go? Ah, there she is," said Jill, spotting the fairy on the clock. "I wonder if she can talk. Can you?"

"Yes, but I'm shy!" said the fairy softly.

Jill was so excited, "She does talk, she really does! There now. It's okay. I won't hurt you."

She tried to encourage the fairy to fly onto her open hand, but it flew up to one of Aphrodite's hair hooks instead. Peter and Paul tweeted in celebration at the fairy's arrival, causing the jack-in-the-box to pop up, at long last.

Jack said, "Careful now Jill. Young fairies are shy. They're very delicate and scare easily. You must be patient. I suggest you leave her alone for a while."

"Are you sure? How do you know that?" asked Jill, as she let the fairy be.

"I'm the wonky controller. I know all about the rules *and* the gifts. It's just what I do," said Jack smugly.

Jill felt a pang of guilt, "Oh Jack, you popped up all by yourself. I'm so sorry, I meant to turn your handle, I really did, but well in all the excitement..."

Jack interrupted her, "Jill I must tell you I really can't be doing with too much excitement anyway. I'd rather keep my head down and pop-up only when I'm needed. That's my job!"

Which was when Edward spoke, "Well I never! You're actually real. My sister *was* telling the truth," he said, still scratching his chin.

"Edward! You can see him. You can see Jack and the fairy! It means you've got your imagination back."

She hugged her brother, tighter than in a very long while.

"Yes Jill, I see them alright," said Edward in a way that suggested he was up to no good!

"And Jack, your face looks different today. It's a surprised face," said Jill.

"Well observed. I'm an emoji in a box... a gesturing jester. My face changes to match my mood," claimed Jack.

Edward was still scratching his chin when he said, "Emoji faces are really cool."

"Just wait until you see my 'two-faced' face Edward," snapped Jack, adding, "I say boy, you look rather sickly. You have the most ghastly dark circles under your eyes. And the scratching, erm, I wonder, could it be?"

"My brother doesn't look sickly. He's just missing his forty winks! Now Jack... I'm really glad you came out. I wanted a word with you. You said if we said that thing we mustn't say about Santa that Christmas would be cancelled, but that was wrong, wasn't it?"

"Hey, you just said, 'forty winks'!" cried Edward.

"Shush Edward. I'm telling Jack off."

"I say, first you ignore me, and now you're telling me off? Fine! As for the Santa thing, it was a small mistake, I admit. It's because of my wonky spring. I can't get everything right."

"Ah yes, the wonky spring. All I really want is for you to say sorry for getting it wrong," said Jill.

"Sorry for getting it wrong?" said Jack sarcastically. Here, let me make it up to you. May I suggest you speak to Aphrodite about Edward's forty winks? She'll know what to do."

Jill nodded. "Okay, we'll ask her," she said, admiring the fairy.

"Jack, I'm scratching because I've a hair growing out of my chin!"

"I feared as much. We'll need to keep an eye on you... a very close eye."

Jill had a thought, "Perhaps it's because you keep trying to click your fingers Edward. Maybe that's to blame for the hair on your chin."

"That's another lie Jill," snapped Edward.

"Little pig, little pig, won't you let me come in, no, no, no, not by the hair on my chinny, chin, chin!" sang Jill.

"You're picking on me again," sobbed Edward.

Jill clicked her fingers several times to tease her brother, causing the candles to get seriously confused. They flickered on and off for ages, which unsettled the poor fairy and sent Jack back inside his box.

***

By the time Aphrodite came home and kicked off her clumpy boots, the candles had finally stopped flashing, but the hair on Edward's chin had grown even longer.

"Sit down child. Let me take a good look at you," said Aphrodite.

Edward did so. He sat on the wingback chair clutching his teddy.

"How spectacular! That hair's curly, white... and as tough as wire," she said, failing miserably to cut it with some nail scissors, so she grabbed some tweezers and tugged away at the little beasty.

"Ouch!" yelped Edward, being yanked forward. "That hurts!"

But it would not budge, not one bit.

"So it won't come off?" said Edward, tearfully, as he rubbed his throbbing chin.

"No Edward. And those terrible bags under your eyes... they won't do at all," said Aphrodite.

"Jack said it's because of the forty winks. He said to ask you about it," said Jill.

"Ah, yes, your forty winks. I'm sorry Edward but I can't do anything about that until tomorrow, I'm afraid. We need what comes out of door five first."

"But I've not been to sleep for four whole nights... four nights... *four*!" he told Teddy. "How am I even alive?"

"Indeed Edward, marvelous isn't it" said Aphrodite. "Time for a quick cuppa and something to nibble. Children, I believe I smell some freshly baked lemon drizzle cake.

DOOR FIVE

On day five Edward took a turn to open one of Archie's doors. He was a sleepy, curly-chin-haired, boy with hope. He slowly opened door five. Inside was a miniature white rocking horse. He took it out carefully and showed his sister, the robins and the, as yet, unnamed fairy.

"It's a little horse," said Edward. "I don't understand. How can that possibly help with my forty winks?"

"Put it down... let's see what happens," suggested Jill.

Edward did so. In a sparkle and flash the rocking horse grew big enough for both children to sit on. It had brown buttons for eyes, a glorious mane and a swishy tail. There were leather reins, a saddle and stirrups. The horse rocked on two curved wooden runners - a little like skis. There was a button on one ear marked 'Press Me', so Edward did just that, but he was disappointed, "I pressed the button on Rocky, but nothing happened."

"Rocky? Oh, so now you've named him as well," said Jill, wagging her finger once more.

"I just came out with it," replied Edward.

"Well I actually like it, so you're lucky. But I'm *definitely* going to pick the fairy's name, deal?"

"Deal!"

Rocky seemed to like his name, for his button eyes blinked and his tail swished.

"Here, let me try the 'Press Me' button," said Jill.

She pressed it. Alas, she had no luck either, but it didn't keep the children from riding Rocky. There was plenty of room for them both on the saddle. Jill held Edward and Edward held the reins. They began rocking gently with, "Trot-on," but were soon cantering, and galloping crying, "Ye-Ha!" and pretending to race Rocky and perform circus tricks.

Kat kept her distance, but Peter and Paul flew from their perches and settled on Rocky's mane.

"Look, they're rocking robins," joked Edward.

Inspired, the fairy bravely flew onto Rocky's tail.

"Wow," cried Jill, looking over her shoulder, "The fairy's landed on Rocky's swishy tail. *Swish*! Swish! I think I'll call her Swish!"

Swish was perfectly happy with that. She celebrated by whispering, "Swish! You get one wish with Swish!" But the children didn't hear her because they were making far too much noise by rocking Rocky so quickly. If they went any faster, they'd be at serious risk of toppling over.

Thankfully, that didn't happen.

When Aphrodite came home the children were still rocking on Rocky. As usual, Aphrodite wore her shaggy coat, boots and sunglasses. She still had antler hair, but her nose wasn't anywhere near as shiny. She was holding a bag full of cotton wool buds and balls.

"Hello my friends, I'm home! I had an extraordinarily quiet day. There's nothing to be done until the post arrives, so I came home early to prepare for my big day. I've much to do here though. Later I'll be cleaning the dirt out of my belly button and getting the wax out of my ears!"

The children giggled so much they almost fell of the horse.

"You are funny," said Jill.

"I aim to please, but do speak up. It's the wax. My ears are blocked," she said, fiddling with an ear.

Aphrodite threw her coat on the floor and kicked off her boots. One almost hit the clock. She put on her slippers. They went well with her Christmas bauble patterned trousers and dazzling gold blouse.

"And we're having tremendous fun," chuckled Jill, "The only problem is Edward's now extra sleepy because of all the rocking."

"Edward's sheepy?" asked Aphrodite.

"No sleepy!" replied Jill loudly.

"Ah, it'll be time for his forty winks. Now Edward, climb down off Rocky and take a seat in my chair... let's move Teddy first. Oh my, his torn ear is barely staying on. Let me see to that," she said, pushing Teddy's torn right ear back into place. "We'll need some super special thread for that!"

Edward sat in the wingback chair and waited for a spring to pop. None did. Aphrodite leaned over him. It was quite a sight.

"Now let's take a look at you. You do look rather sickly, a little green I'd say. Terrible dark circles and that hair growing out of your chin... ooh my, that's now a whopper... right it's easy-peasy, all you need to do is wink forty times and all will be well. Watch me, left eye, then right eye, and so on," said Aphrodite winking.

"Are you serious? That's ridiculous," said Jill.

"It's Saint Nicholas? Where? He is very early," replied Aphrodite. She looked up at the lounge window to check if he was there.

"No. I said, *'ridiculous!'*"

"Ah, I'm the mistress in the art of ridiculousness. Now, shall we begin... oh and don't forget to count aloud as you go."

Edward winked each eye in turn, counting as he went, "One, two, three, four, five..."

Kat nodded her head in rhythm with the counting.

"Twenty-two, twenty-three, twenty-four... no, it's *not* working. I'm still awake," he said disappointed.

"No, no, no. You can't start talking when you're counting. It's not how it's done. Start again from the beginning... and only say the numbers."

So Edward counted afresh, winking each eye in turn as the robin's whistled in time with the numbers. Edward counted all the way through, "thirty-six, thirty-seven, thirty-eight, thirty-nine, *forty*!" Bingo! Edward's head fell forward and he gave out the loudest SNORE his sister had ever heard, then he woke up again, and that was that!

Aphrodite rubbed her hands together in celebration, "There... as welcome as a snowdrop at Christmas and look, no more bags under your eyes."

"I'm wide awake!" chirped Edward.

"That's so ridiculous," said Jill once more.

Jack-in-the-box chose his moment well. He popped up with a winking eye on a cheeky face. "Ta-da!" he said, just as a magician would at the end of a trick.

Swish celebrated too. "Swish! Swish!" she cried, flying just above them.

"Now children, I think it's time to clear the wax from my ears!"

The children covered their eyes, but were really glad to hear Aphrodite's footsteps climbing the stairs, holding the bag of cotton wool.

DOOR SIX

With Jill's fingers wrapped around Edward's, the children pulled the handle on door six together. Inside they found three model carol singers in old-fashioned clothes holding hymn sheets. There was a girl and two boys, one of whom had broken legs. Carefully, they put the carol singers down and waited for the sparkle and the flash, but it didn't come. Instead, the out of time clock chimed... dong, dong, dong, dong, dong, DONG! The last of the chimes was louder and startled Swish and the robins. They flew from their perches and circled the lounge chirping and swishing, teasing Kat who made strange 'mit-mit' sounds as she watched them fly.

"Shush Swish, Peter, Paul, don't be afraid. It's just the clock chiming," said Jill.

The excitement brought Jack out of his box. He had a thinking face, "Wrong! Unlikely as it may seem, the clock chimes when new guests knock loudly on the front door. The polite thing to do in such circumstances is open it."

The children hurried to the front door. Kat stopped making her strange cat cries and followed them. She was at their feet when the door opened. Outside were three carol singers in old-fashioned clothing, winter hats and coats. Their mouths were wide open ready to burst into song, so far open that it was almost possible to see their tonsils.

"La-la, la-la, la!" sang the girl, warming up. She had an enchanting voice and large soulful green eyes with thick fluttering lashes. Red ringlets of hair dangled free from a black bonnet tied under her chin. On her left was a chubby cherub of a boy with wispy blond hair. On her right was a gangly kid in a beaten-up old wheelchair. Both the boys had robins on their shoulders.

"Ready," said the girl, and they began to sing, "O come all ye faithful, joyful and triumphant. O come ye, O come ye to... to... to..."

And there they stopped open-mouthed, unable, oddly, to complete the simple verse, as the rest of the lyrics were missing from their hymn books.

Kat did her best to help. She cried, "Meow-yow-yow," to finish the line for them.

Jill sensed the singers weren't ready to give up. "Once more?" she suggested.

"Yes, try again!" said Edward.

So they did, "O come, all ye faithful, joyful and triumphant. O come ye, O come ye to... to... to..."

Kat repeated, "Meow-yow-yow" turned up her nose and wandered back into the cottage.

It was all very bizarre. The singers stood on the doorstep looking rather embarrassed.

"I'm sorry," said the girl, "It's never happened before. I can't begin to explain it."

"I think it's because the words are lost and so are we," said the chubby boy.

"You're lost?" asked Edward. "That happened to us too. You must be in the same dream."

"A dream, eh, well Carol believes we're just on an adventure," said the gangly boy.

"Whose Carol?" asked Jill.

"I am," said the girl.

"We've been round and round in circles in those woods. I wouldn't trust those signs – this way and that! Is this your house?" asked the gangly boy.

"No, we're just visiting," said Jill. She whispered in Edward's ear. He nodded. She turned and asked the singers, "Would you all like to come in? We've tea and biscuits."

The singers glanced about at all the trees surrounding the cottage. They didn't really have much of a choice.

"I'm Jill, and this is Edward. I'm his big sister. We have robins too."

"I'm Nigel," said the gangly boy in a wheelchair.

"And I'm Gordon. Is that lemon puff biscuits I can smell?" asked the plump boy.

"Probably," said Edward, "Come in, quickly now before the Christmas Grumps grab you," he joked.

The singers came into the cottage and hung up their coats and things on pegs by the door. Oddly, a few new ones had appeared after the clock had chimed.

Jill told them, "Please speak quietly because of Swish, she's a Christmas fairy and doesn't like loud noises... we also have Rocky the Rocking Horse."

"Oh, so that's why the sign said, 'Knock Here Quietly," said Gordon.

"A Christmas fairy, in this house? I was hoping it was so," said Carol.

"And I like your jumper," Gordon told Jill, "It has a Christmas pudding on it. I do love Christmas pudding."

They went into the lounge. Carol took a good look around. "My, this is... cosy. Oh, there she is. It's a real fairy? She's so beautiful," she said. Carol was wearing a long crimson dress which flared out at the bottom. It had a stiff collared neck.

Jack was already out of his box. "Yes she's real, but shy, so be patient with her. *Hmm*, so, everyone gets introduced except me? I may live in a clown's box but I came out of door number one. Yes. I'm *Top of the Pops*... pop pickers!"

Carol took to Jack immediately, "How wonderful. You can speak!" She knelt down, "Now let me guess, you might be Jack?" she asked curiously.

"Carol, don't jump to conclusions. Appearances can be deceptive. I for one won't judge you by those enormous eyes and lashes, they're so dreamy! Pinch me I'm dreaming," said Jack teasingly.

"For me it feels more like an adventure than a dream," said Carol, fluttering her eyelashes at him.

Jack admitted, "Okay, I'm Jack, and yes you're correct, this too is an adventure. Congratulations Little Miss Psychic Pants. I hope this day finds you well. I would be more than happy to help with the conundrum... your little carol problem... you know the 'to... to... to' thing but my memory isn't what it once was. It's my wonky spring you see. It drives me around the twist."

"My spring's wonky too," said Nigel sadly. He was stylishly dressed with a red bow tie, shirt and jacket.

"I like your bow tie," said Jill, "It's bang-on."

"Thanks Jill. It's just fancy dress though," replied Nigel.

Gordon was wearing a tightly-fitting faded lemon shirt that was buttoned all the way up to his neck and a pair of smart brown trousers.

None of the carol singers looked very comfortable in their clothes. It was a strange thing indeed, for nobody could help them with the 'to, to, to' conundrum. Try as they might not one person could remember how to finish the verse from the famous carol.

"Perhaps Aphrodite can help. She should be home soon," said Edward.

"*Aphrodite*? The Greek goddess of beauty?" asked Carol.

"Precisely! That's just what I said," replied Jill.

"She's eh, lovely but weird. We definitely think she's fibbing about her name though," said Edward.

"Pretending Edward, there's a difference remember."

Kat flapped her ears and curled her tail.

"And watch Kat, she's listening to us," claimed Edward.

"And what about the cat? You didn't tell us her name," said Carol.

"Oh, she's just called Kat!" replied Jill.

"The pussycat is called *Kat*?" said Gordon, smirking and shaking his head.

"Aphrodite said Kat is short for Katrina," said Edward.

"What's new pussycat?" asked Carol.

Kat cried, "Meow-e-ow-ow-o."

The children giggled.

***

When Aphrodite came home she was holding a surprise for the children. She stood in the cramped hall, fiddling with something when she called, "Hello Jill. Hello Edward, I'm home. Have you missed me? My ears are all squeaky clean now so I've borrowed the wind-up gramophone and a box of records... we had them in the good old days before CDs and downloading the streams. You see, I need to practice my dancing and singing for the big day. It'll be good for Swish too. Young fairies are calmed by music."

She stomped into the lounge, and threw her coat in the only available space. She kicked off her boots and put her reindeer slippers on. She was wearing Christmas pudding pattern trousers and a forest-green blouse.

"Ooh, Jill we have matching tops and bottoms. How delicious! And there you three are. Welcome Carol, Nigel and Gordon. You're all looking very... spiffing... and luscious lashes, what a lovely gown you have, so elegant. Now, first things first, the gold sparkly toothbrush is mine. Edward's is red and Jill's is green."

"I thought *mine* was gold!" shrieked Jill.

"Did I say that, oh? Anyway, the others are blue, purple and orange. I'll let you decide which you prefer, please use them. We don't want to lose our teeth, not in this house. Now, we'll all have to squeeze in a bit, but it'll be fine, you'll see. Besides, I'm starting a high-fibre diet tomorrow as I need to lose a few pounds for my big day... so that'll make a bit more room."

"Aphrodite, what's a high fibre diet?" asked Edward.

"I'll be eating lots of green vegetables, soggy sprouts mostly!" she replied enthusiastically.

All the children giggled.

Carol was still chuckling when she said, "Sprouts, oh. Look you're all so wonderful and we..." But Aphrodite interrupted her, "Stop, you're staying and that's that. I'm positively not explaining it all again. I'll leave that to Jill and Edward."

"But where will they sleep?" asked Edward, "The cottage only has three bedrooms and three beds?"

Aphrodite knew just what to say, "*Does it*? Children please. The cottage always finds a way. I suggest you take a fresh look upstairs."

So they did. There was now a bunk bed and a single bed in one room and two single beds in the other. They each had nice new duvets and there wasn't a sheet or blanket to be seen.

"It's absolutely ridiculous!" shrieked Jill, when the girls came back downstairs.

"It's magical, is what it is," said Aphrodite. "But, I did say we needed to squeeze in a bit, didn't I? You'll have to share I'm afraid. You'll find a 'No Children Allowed' sign on my bedroom door. Kat will let me know if you go in there. She'll leave me a nice new scratch on the door frame," said Aphrodite. She glared at Jill and Edward. They blushed. Now they really were looking sheepish!

Carol thought of a problem, "This is all too kind of you, but what about Nigel? How will he..."

Aphrodite interrupted again, "Oh, worry not for Rocky will see to it! He's full of party tricks. He has reins and stirrups. Nigel can ride him up and down the stairs."

"But my legs don't work. How will I get on and off?" asked Nigel.

"It's easy-peasy... you just say 'Rocky On' to ride him and 'Rocky Off' to dismount."

"Rocky on?" replied Nigel, which teleported him to the saddle, with his feet safely strapped into the stirrups. "Oh my, I won't fall off will I?" he asked nervously.

"No chance of that. Rocky will look after you, I promise you... and to get him to move just say, 'walk on' and so on, like you would with a real horse, but Rocky only works his magic for you, Nigel."

"Aww!" said the other children disappointedly, except Carol, who was thrilled. "How fabulous, a cottage that grows, a talking jack-in-the-box, a fairy and a magical rocking horse," she said with a beaming smile.

Gordon saw things a little differently. "It's amazing, but impossible," he said, hands in pockets.

Jack put him right, "Improbable yes, but nothing's impossible at Conjuring Cottage!"

"So that's the cottage's name, is it?" said Edward, "But what does conjuring mean?"

"I suggest you add a dictionary to your Santa list this year! Oh I forgot. You don't believe in him anymore, do you?" said Jack sarcastically.

Carol was shocked. "*You don't believe in Father Christmas*?" she asked.

"It's not easy for me," replied Edward sadly. He toyed with the white hair coiled-up under his chin.

Jack mocked him, saying in a squeaky voice, "It's not easy for me!" Then in his normal voice he said, "The verb 'to conjure' means to make something appear by magic, or as if by magic, thus Conjuring Cottage is a place where magic happens! *Ta-da*."

Nigel began to rock slowly on the horse, "Wow! A place where magic happens, real magic. I wonder..."

Aphrodite calmed his enthusiasm. "There are rules. Let's not get our hopes up," she said.

Swish flew over to Nigel. Fairies, even very young ones, have a habit of knowing when people need them the most. She settled on Nigel's shoulder next to his rocking robin.

"What do you mean rules?" asked Carol.

Incredibly, in all the excitement, they hadn't asked or been told about Archie the Advent Calendar. Door six on the wooden Christmas tree was still open, but little did Carol and her singers know they had arrived because of it. It was probably wise to leave that for another day, which was just what Aphrodite suggested, "The rules are part of the adventure, but we've had more than enough enchantment for one day. Jack will explain it all in the morning."

"Bright and early, if you please," urged Jack. He shut his lid, believing his job was done for the day.

Carol asked, "Do I get to share a bedroom with Jill?"

"No, sorry, I'd rather share with my brother," said Jill.

"I can't share with them, *they're boys*!" insisted Carol.

"Well Edward's *my brother*!"

"But I don't mind. It's not fair to make her share with them," said Edward.

Jill wasn't at all impressed, "Be quiet Edward!" she demanded.

Aphrodite put a stop to it, "You lost children, always squabbling. It's like listening to a broken record. Besides, the Conjuring Cottage has already decided. I think you'll find the bedroom doors have your names on them."

The children dashed back upstairs to check. It was true. Jill and Carol were sharing and so were the boys.

"*Fine*..." muttered Jill, when they returned.

"Good, now, that's settled let's have some fun, shall we?" suggested Aphrodite. She marched over to the front door and bolted it tightly. "That's to keep the happiness in and the Christmas Grumps out," she said, before putting the gramophone on a table. She selected a record, pulled it from the sleeve, placed it on the record player and turned the crank handle.

Jack popped up with an emoji heart face, "Oh my... she's turning the handle! I'm in love... with another music making machine!"

The children all giggled.

The first record was, 'Jumping Jack Flash'. As it played, Jill clicked her fingers many times over which made the candles switch on and off like disco lights.

The other children clicked their fingers too, except poor Edward. Aphrodite chose some other amusing songs, including 'What's New Pussycat' and 'Rocking Robin'. Rocky joined in the fun with Nigel grooving on his back. Swish loved the music and danced like a ballerina, until Aphrodite changed the mood, "Oh Carol and her singers, this one's for you," she said, putting another record on. It played, "O come all ye faithful, joyful and triumphant. O come ye, O come ye to… to… to…"

Aphrodite interrupted, "Oh my, the record's scratched. How fantabulous!"

DOOR SEVEN

Edward took the top bunk, but still couldn't sleep, so passed the night twiddling his curly chin hair and failing miserably to click his fingers. He spent almost every waking minute listening to Nigel snore and Gordon grunt in their sleep. Frustrated, he got out of bed, pulled back the curtains and looked out of the window into the night. In the woods beyond, pairs of glowing orange eyes stared right back at him in the darkness, but Edward wasn't afraid, not one bit.

As he watched them, the hair on his chin tingled. Now and again, he thought he saw strange stumpy figures on the move.

"I don't like Christmas, not one bit," he whispered.

Edward watched them for hours before eventually returning to his bed to cuddle Teddy. When dawn finally arrived, he counted out his forty winks then dozed off. BOOM! A gigantic snore shook the room. It woke his new friends and scared their robins away, though quite how the birds fled the cottage was a mystery. There again, it was a house of magic.

In the other bedroom, Aphrodite had given the girls an empty super-sized matchbox to use as a bed for Swish. They added a rolled up sock for a comfy pillow and made a cosy cover from a folded pillowcase. Swish had slept soundly until Edward snored. Frightened, she swished about the room frantically, knocking some small books from their shelves and scaring Jill's robin away. It seems Aphrodite was spot on about fairies not liking loud noises!

***

All the children were in their dressing gowns and slippers when they came down for breakfast. Edward was in the kitchen curious about an old metal saucepan on the cooker. He flipped the saucepan lid and found inside some disgusting cold soggy Brussels sprouts. A ghastly smell went right up Edward's nostrils and all the way into his brain. He gulped.

"Oh, what's that *revolting* smell?" asked Jill, pinching her nose.

"They're... cough... Brussels sprouts... from Aphrodite's high-fibre diet," replied Edward. Unable to resist them, he put his hand right inside the pan.

"Stop it Edward," said Jill firmly. "You can't possibly have sprouts for breakfast."

"But I don't want to eat them. I only want to touch them and feel how squidgy they are."

"That's a big fat *no* Edward!"

Yet, before he replaced the lid, Edward secretly dipped a finger in the cold squidgy sprouts and sucked it clean. He actually rather liked it!

About the breakfast table were some extra chairs, a space for Nigel, and twice as much food than before. Gordon couldn't get enough of the honey and pancakes, "These are so delicious," he said, unaware that honey dribbled down his chin and on to his lemon shirt.

"Where's Aphrodite?" asked Carol, tucking into a pancake.

"Oh she does that. She's never here in the morning. I warned you she was a bit weird," said Edward.

"I kind of like weird," replied Carol, "Who wants to be normal, whatever that is? Anyhow, yesterday she said something about rules... and that Jack could explain everything."

"That's the rules to Archie's Advent Adventure," said Jill.

"Ah, the adventure, cool. But who's Archie?" Carol replied.

"Archie's the magical Advent calendar," said Jill, "It's how we got Jack, Swish, Rocky and... eh... and... and a robin came out of it too. Jack told me the rules... but gets in a muddle. We have to open a new door each day until Christmas. It's my turn next."

"Do show me," urged Carol. She leapt off the chair and skipped into the lounge. The others followed quickly and gathered about Archie. Kat crept out from under Aphrodite's armchair and sat amongst them purring.

"So Archie's the wooden Christmas tree," said Carol, "I had a feeling about that."

Jill found door number seven and happily tugged at the handle. However, inside was just a plain old mince pie. "Oh, how disappointing," said Jill. "It has the number seven on it, but I was hoping for something more exciting to show you..."

"I'm not disappointed. It smells delicious. Can I have it?" asked Gordon, reaching out for the pie.

"No, you mustn't. Jack said that we absolutely must *not* eat any of Archie's gifts," stressed Jill.

"Are you sure? I do love a mince pie," he said ogling it.

"I'm totally sure. We had a Santa Sweet in door two, but didn't eat that either, did we Edward?" said Jill.

Edward fidgeted and said, "Eh, no... and I don't like boiled sweets or hard toffee."

"Where is it Edward? The Santa Sweet? I've not seen it since," she asked.

"Eh... I was going to talk to you about that."

"What are you saying? There's a rule that says we mustn't lose any of the gifts. Have you lost it Edward?"

"I'm sorry. I can't remember where I put it," he said glumly.

Jack came out of his box. He had a dismayed rolling eyes face, "So you've lost the Santa Sweet have you Edward? I despair. Jill is correct, under rule three you'll need to find it before Christmas Day or Christmas will be lost... forever."

"Christmas lost forever?" asked Gordon.

"All because of a sweet? That can't be right," said Nigel, fiddling with his bow-tie.

"Rules are rules," said Jack.

"And rule three has three bits," added Jill. "It also says we must use the gifts wisely and that we can't repair anything that's broken."

"So broken things can't be fixed?" said Nigel sadly.

Jack was a bit muddled, "Did I say that? I guess I did."

"Jack, you're making it up as you're going along. It's not fair," said Edward. He was getting tearful. "I *didn't* lose the sweet. I just put it somewhere but can't remember where." He grabbed his teddy for comfort, and hugged him tightly.

"No Edward, I'm not making it up. It's definitely one of the Santa clauses."

"The Santa clauses?" asked Carol curiously.

"Oh it's too confusing. Clauses are rules, just think of it that way," said Jill.

Jack disagreed, "I'm not befuddled by it. Anyway children, just make sure you keep that mince pie safe. Delicious as it might be, not a single nibble for anyone. Is that clear Gordon?"

"But it's only a mince pie! What harm can it do?" he asked.

"Now don't be greedy Gordon," urged Jack.

Edward held up his Teddy and said, "Jack... Teddy has an idea. He says, 'If you're so worried about the mince pie getting eaten, then why not look after it yourself?'"

"Me, but I might get crumbs in my box. I can't be doing with crumbs. They're so uncomfortable."

Carol spoke, "Edward, I think that's a really excellent idea. I doubt Jack eats anything, do you Jack? So it'll be perfectly safe with him."

"That's right. He doesn't eat, do you Jack? Oh, Carol, how did you know that?" asked Jill.

"I just did," she replied.

Jill was becoming suspicious of Carol and mumbled, "What *is* she up to?"

"It's not against the rules to rule it out... so, okay, I'll do it," said Jack. "I'll look after the pie."

With the mince pie in Jack's safe hands, or should that be under his spring, the children got dressed and began another search of Conjuring Cottage to look for the missing sweet. Edward was so eager to find it he left his teddy on Aphrodite's chair before joining in. Together they searched high and low and inside and out, but without any joy. There was only one place left to look, Aphrodite's bedroom, but Kat was guarding her door.

Edward hesitated, "We can't go in remember, 'No Children Allowed'. Aphrodite will know because Kat will scratch the door frame. I'm not going in. I don't want to get in even more trouble."

But Jill said, "The sweet must be in her room. We went in there that day remember. Lock Kat in somewhere while I look around. She won't know we've been in there then. You go downstairs and keep watch. I'll be super quick. If Aphrodite returns while I'm in her room, distract her."

"How? What will I say?"

"Make something up!"

"But you're better at telling fibs than I am," said Edward.

"Just do as I say please. We need to get the sweet back don't we?" snapped Jill.

Carol tried to reassure Edward. "Don't worry Edward, I'm sure it'll be fine," she said.

Kat flapped her ears, which led Edward to say, "*See*, Kat's listening. I wouldn't do it if I were you. I'm sure it's not in there."

But Jill ignored her brother. She locked Kat in the bathroom and left her meowing in protest. Jill went into Aphrodite's room alone. She searched it very carefully doing her best to put things back just as she found them. She noticed some new scented candles, Sneaky Cheeky and Smiling Happy Faces. There were more ticks on the Big Day list, and new tasks added such as, 'cut toe nails,' 'flying lessons' and 'a sad goodbye'.

Jill whispered to herself, "Flying lessons and a sad goodbye? Aphrodite, what does this mean?"

There was a book lying on the bed called 'Good Elf or Bad'. Curious, she skipped through some pages. There were pictures of elves up to terrible mischief and sentences like, 'You can never really trust an elf.' She put the book down and looked under the bed. She found several photograph albums and pulled one out. The first page was headed 1986. There were pictures of children named Clare and Nicholas with robins on their shoulders. There was a fairy, an elf giving a 'thumbs up', Rocky, and a black cat.

She flipped forward to 1988. There were different children but similar photos. There were also drawings and cards from children. One read, 'To Aphrodite, thank you, for making us so happy'. Another read, 'Extra special Lady' and 'Thank you for helping us go home.'

She flipped forward a few pages. On 1991 were different children but similar photos and cards. 1994 had more of the same. She tried another album. It was the same for 2009 and similar for 2012, 2016 and so on.

Jill whispered, “Wow! When children dream of Christmas so many dream of Aphrodite! I never knew she was so loved.” She wiped away a tear. Only then did she hear Aphrodite’s voice just outside the door. Quickly, Jill squeezed under the bed, making sure none of the photo albums were sticking out. She heard the bedroom door open and watched Aphrodite’s reindeer slippers walk about the room. Aphrodite reached the bed and sat down. The bed springs creaked and bowed and squashed Jill. She could just about breathe!

Aphrodite fidgeted on the bed. She began to read aloud, “Elves come in all shapes and sizes and from every country and corner of the world. Most of them are really helpful, kind and brilliant at creating and making things. They work hard and seldom complain. Be thankful if you have elves like this.” She fidgeted again then continued, “Sometimes though, elves can be very naughty indeed. You can never really tell if your elf has a dark side until it’s too late. It comes as a terrible shock. Keep on your toes. There’s one clue to their true personality and it’s this... a fairy instinctively knows. If a fairy isn’t an elves friend beware.”

Aphrodite put down the book. She fidgeted some more. Her slippers hit the floor again. She stood up and broke wind, LOUDLY. The sound and the smell went all the way through her poor Christmas penguins leggings. They would need to go in the wash!
“Oh dear, far too many sprouts,” she said chuckling.

Jill really struggled not to burst out laughing. She put her hand over her mouth just as Aphrodite did it again, then once more. It was no laughing matter now. Jill pinched her nose as tightly as could be because the stink was so horrid.

Aphrodite mumbled, “Oh my, I need to visit the bathroom.” She grabbed the jar for the Soggy Sprout Farts scented candle and made straight for the bathroom. It was Jill’s one chance to escape. She scrambled out from under the bed, sped past Kat, who was busy marking the door frame with a scratch, and dashed down the stairs into the lounge.

The other children had been waiting anxiously for her. They saw the troubled look on Jill's face. "She caught you didn't she? I told you *not* to go in there," Edward said. "But you didn't listen, did you?"

"No, she didn't catch me *actually*," said Jill smugly.

"Okay then, did you find the Santa Sweet?" asked Edward.

"No."

"See, I told you I didn't leave it in there," he said.

Jill just shook her head. She may have escaped but Jack realised something wasn't quite right, "What's wrong?" he asked.

"Nothing!"

"There is, I can tell. I'm your brother. What happened?" he asked.

"How about this, you tell me why you don't believe in Santa anymore, and I'll tell you what I saw?" snapped Jill.

"Ooh that was close, you nearly said it again! But I can't tell you and you're just being mean."

"Don't talk to me about being mean, Edward. I'm just looking after you. It's what I do, remember," said Jill.

The other children didn't know what to say and didn't want to get involved in the argument. When Aphrodite eventually came downstairs she found the children sitting in silence and looking miserable. She'd expected as much and was carrying a pair of 'Sneaky Cheeky' and 'Smiling Happy Faces' scented candles. She put them over the fireplace and clicked her fingers. "That's much better," she said. Before they knew it the children couldn't help but smile again.

DOOR EIGHT

In the morning, Jill grabbed some toast and sat on the sofa to eat her breakfast. Still wearing her dressing gown and slippers, she'd laid out paper and colouring pencils on the coffee table. Kat was playfully tapping the pencils and watching them roll off the table, when Edward came in and asked, "Why are you eating breakfast in here? Are you still annoyed with me for losing the Santa Sweet?"

"No Edward. I just need to get on with this. You should make one too, she deserves it," said Jill, as she folded a sheet of paper in two and started drawing.

"But what are you doing?" asked Edward.

"I'm making a 'Thank You' card. It's for Aphrodite."

"Why? Are we leaving? I thought you didn't like her. You said she was a witch." He sat down next to Jill, picked up one of the pencils and began teasing Kat with it.

"Edward, I was wrong. I know now why her name is Aphrodite. It's because she's beautiful on the inside," she said warmly.

Kat flapped her ears and curled her tail, just as Carol and the boys joined them.

"Oh you're drawing. Is that a Christmas tree?" asked Carol.

Jill nodded and began to colour the needles green, "I want it ready for when Aphrodite comes home."

"Do you know where she goes to each day?" Carol asked, running her fingers through the pencils, "I've a feeling it's somewhere amazing."

"I've been wondering that too and about her Big Day. Perhaps she's getting married?" asked Edward.

Everyone looked back at him as if to say, 'Are you kidding?' Everyone except Jill.

Nigel had an idea, "Why don't we follow her and find out where she goes?"

"Yeah, that would be epically sneaky and cheeky," said Gordon, chuckling.

Kat gave a pencil a really mean swipe then flapped her ears again.

***

After the card was finished, Jill was ready for door number eight. She opened it and looked inside. There were six neatly stacked wooden alphabet blocks. As she took them out, the blocks slipped from her hand. Whilst they fell and tumbled on the rug they grew larger. They settled in an uneven line and spelt, 'S, -, C, R, -, T' because the letter E's were so faded they could barely be seen.

"Wow! That's awesome. They've spelt '*secret*'!" said Edward, "Here, let me have a try."

He gathered up the blocks and rolled them on the rug. They fell into line and spelt the word, 'F, A, T, H, -, R'.

"Father? Why father? What can that mean?" said Edward, puzzled.

"Here, let me have a turn?" asked Carol. Without waiting for a reply, she picked up the blocks and rolled them again. This time they read, 'P, I, -, C, -, S'. "Pieces? Hmm," said Carol. She had a feeling about what that meant, but kept it to herself.

Jack had been listening to every word. He came out of his box with a poking-out tongue face. “Tardy today aren’t we?” he said.

“Hey Jack. We’re late because I’ve been drawing,” replied Jill.

“Ah, a picture of me I hope. Did you get my good side?”

“What with your tongue hanging out! No, another time Jack. Here, I drew Archie, look,” she said showing Jack her picture. “And, we got some alphabet blocks out of today’s door.”

“When I rolled them they read ‘pieces’”, said Carol.

“Yes, I heard. ‘Pieces’ yes, well that’s what you three children are. In Archie’s Advent Adventure, you aren’t players, but pieces. You can still open his calendar doors, but I really wouldn’t recommend it.”

"So we're only part of the game, and that's it?" asked Carol.

"I'm afraid so. It's because you came out of door six," said Jack coldly,

"Oh they haven't told you yet, have they?"

"Door six? The stupid bricks should have read *unfair* because that's what it is. And I remember you said broken pieces can't be fixed!" said Nigel, as he glared at his wheelchair.

"Well, I don't want to play this game anymore," said Gordon, sulking.

"We were going to tell you about door six, but we were just waiting for the right moment," said Jill quietly.

"It's fine. We'll just have to make the most of it," said Carol.

Jack came to her aid, "That's the spirit luscious lashes! Remember, the number six is a perfect number. It is a symbol of completeness and beauty, which says everything about you really, everything!"

Though, in truth, the Carol singers didn't care much for the rest of the rules to Archie's Advent Adventure. Instead, they took to playing at cards and working their way through the board games until Aphrodite returned. When she did and kicked off her clumpy boots one struck the alphabet blocks. They tumbled and spelt, 'B, -, A, U, T, Y'.

Aphrodite chuckled, "Ah children, the alphabet blocks never lie! It's so wonderful to see you all again, even if there's a strong smell of Sneaky Cheeky in here. What have you been up to? I shall have to consult with Kat. 'How was my day?' still no mail! I've twiddled my thumbs so much that they just can't stop... watch."

Her thumbs twiddled furiously with nails painted in shades of smudged green, red and gold polish.

"Look, they're twiddling so fast, I believe I may fly yet!" she said, cheerfully.

Kat couldn't take her eyes of the spinning thumbs. She wriggled her bottom ready to pounce.

"Kat? No!" said Aphrodite firmly, and began to hum the tune to 'Two Little Dickie Birds' and sung the last few words, "Come back Peter, come back Paul."

Her words encouraged Swish to fly in circles about her and returning robins to fly through the front door, which then gently closed itself so as not to frighten Swish. The birds flew to Jill and Edward's shoulders, tweeting merrily. Aphrodite's thumbs stopped twiddling.

"Children, take note. That's how to call your robins back," she said. Proud of her efforts, Aphrodite slumped heavily in her chair. Another spring popped. Boing! She leant forward to check for damage, "That's three broken spring's and counting. Ooh, now I think I'm stuck fast. The cushion has sunk." She desperately tried to wriggle clear, but failed. It was no use. She stood up with the chair wrapped about her bottom. "Oh bother. Do you think it'll catch on?" she asked.

All the children giggled.

DOOR NINE

At breakfast the children enjoyed croissants, crumpets and more delicious pancakes with syrup. Nigel was still extremely curious about Aphrodite's whereabouts each morning, "Maybe Swish could follow Aphrodite!" he suggested, but the girls weren't at all keen on the idea.

"I've a feeling we'll find out soon enough," said Carol. "And whatever it is, I'm sure it's something incredibly important."

"Besides, Swish might get scared and fly away, and we don't want that," added Jill. "Anyway, Aphrodite is probably taking flying lessons. I saw it on her Big Day list."

Carol wasn't sure, "Flying lessons? But yesterday she said something about the mail. You don't need to wait for the mail to learn to fly, do you?"

Edward had an idea, "I know, let's ask the alphabet blocks. They might tell us where she goes!"

They all dashed into the lounge. Edward grabbed the blocks and was about to tumble them.

"Good morning children!" said Aphrodite brightly. The children shrieked with surprise. Aphrodite was sat in her armchair, supported by another cushion. Kat was sat on her lap and Swish was whispering in her ear. The children hadn't expected Aphrodite to be there. Startled, Edward dropped the blocks. They spelt, 'B, O, T, H, - , R'.

"Aphrodite? You're there in your chair? We thought..." said Edward uneasily.

"It's just you..." mumbled Jill.

Aphrodite interrupted, "Bother! The letters spelt 'bother'. I was rather hoping it would be otherwise. Children, would you be so kind and please open door nine now. I always watch when door nine is opened. It's just a precaution. We can't be too careful. You never can tell you see and Christmas itself may depend upon it."

Everyone held their breath as Edward grabbed Teddy then opened door nine. He found the courage to look inside. A sprite figure leapt out. It was a Christmas elf. When he landed he grew to a height just right to sit on a shelf. He was an elegant fellow, dressed in green with large pointy ears and a pointy hat.

"I'm free! Thank my lucky stars. Phew!" said the elf in a cheeky little voice.

He danced a celebratory jig, and sang the names of Santa's reindeer, "Dasher, Dancer, Prancer, Vixen, Comet, Cupid, Donner, Blitzen," before pointing a bony finger at Aphrodite's slippers, "and Rudolf."

"Well done elf. It *is* Rudolf!" said Aphrodite, "So you know the reindeer then?"

"In a funny sort of way, yes I do."

"Stupendous! Welcome elf. Could you tell us your name?" asked Aphrodite.

"Why yes, I'm Master Alf the Elf," he said, bowing and doffing his pointy hat.

Aphrodite sang a little ditty, "An elf called Alf. Alf is an elf. Elfie Alf. Alfie the Elfie sits on a shelfie."

"Very amusing!" replied Alf, clearly unimpressed.

"It's no worse than Ed and Ted. Teddy and Eddie. A Teddy for Edward. Tedward for short," said Aphrodite.

"Not again," mumbled Edward.

"So *you're* Edward. I've heard so much about you," said Alf. He skipped over to him, "You're the talk of Tinsel Town. And there's your teddy. Oh, his little ear has almost fallen off."

"And you're Alf... a real life elf. That's amazing," replied Edward, "Why am I the talk of Tinsel Town, whatever that is, there's nothing special about me? I'm just a lost boy, and I don't much like Christmas anyway."

Aphrodite explained, "Tinsel Town is where the elves live, well most of them anyway."

Nigel was thrilled, "So you're one of Santa's little helpers. Do you make the toys?" he asked, sat upon Rocky.

"Nope, elves don't make toys, we craft them. There's a big difference, huge!" said Alf, stretching out his arms to make his point.

Gordon was confused, "Craft them? I don't understand. How does that work?"

"It's simple. We know in our hearts what each child desires and we craft it in our head."

Carol spoke, "That's really beautiful. I just knew that's how the elves did it."

"That's not all Big Eyes. Some extra special elves repair and reuse old toys. They make them as good as new again," said Alf. "They're whacky inventors too, turning old junk into some super crazy stuff!" He celebrated their expertise by performing a cartwheel but bumped into Jack's box.

Jack came out. He had a suspicious face, "Oh it's an elf. Mischievous and devious. Can never really be trusted. Take a look at the alphabet blocks. They spelt the word 'bother', didn't they? Best put him on the shelf and keep him there I'd say."

Alf patted Jack's head, "They're actually *elf-abet* blocks Jack. And I'd rather be sat on a shelf than stuck in a little box. It can't be much of a view, can it? Oh and I see your spring is wonky," he said sarcastically.

"Leave my spring out of this. It's not my fault it's broken. And I happen to be rather fond of my box."

"Ooh, can I smell mince pies? I do love a mince pie. They're yummy," said Alf, sniffing the air.

"I'm sorry but you're not allowed to eat it," said Gordon, "None of us are."

"So hands off," said Jack firmly.

Alf crossed his arms, shook his head and tutted. He went over to Rocky and Nigel. He climbed up on the horse and tried the 'Press Me' button. It still didn't work. He sat on the saddle in front of Nigel and spotted Jill, "And you young lady must be Jill. You're quiet. What's up Kat got your tongue?"

Kat flapped her ears and curled her tail.

"No, I'm just thinking. I go quiet when I'm thinking," she said, toying with her fringe.

So Alf ignored her and waved at Swish instead, "Ooh a Christmas fairy. What's her name?"

"She's called Swish. I named her," said Jill.

Swish flew up to Alf, sniffed him with her tiny button nose and smiled.

"It's a joy to meet you little teeny-weeny Swish," said Alf, holding out his bony finger to tickle her tummy.

All seemed well, but Aphrodite wasn't taking any chances, "Jill, could you kindly roll the elf-abet blocks. Let's see what they have to say."

"Ooh this will be fun. They'll tell you I'm superb, a marvel or a genius, just you see," said Alf as he leapt off Rocky and hopped over to the blocks.

Jill picked them up and rolled them. She was surprised when they spelt, 'O, R, P, H, A, N'.

"An orphan," said Jill.

"I should have guessed. A child with no parents," said Carol.

"Happy now?" asked Alf, as he jumped over to Aphrodite.

"Happy? Me? Come now Alf, Happy is my middle name. And yes, everything is just as I expected. You're a cheeky little fellow, but you'll do. That's all settled then. I'd best be off. Duty calls."

Aphrodite grabbed her sunglasses, shaggy coat and boots and left. Gordon wanted to follow her, but said nothing. It was an opportunity missed. He feared they might never get such a good chance again.

In the afternoon, Alf entertained the children by cheating during games of Snakes and Ladders, hiding chess pieces and doing card tricks. He amused them greatly. That night Alf the elf slept on the shelf. When Aphrodite clicked the candles out, Alf had a cheeky grin on his face. *What had he got planned*?

***

Upstairs the girls' were tucked up in bed, but Carol couldn't sleep, "Are you awake?" she whispered.

"I am, why?" replied Jill.

"I need to tell you something. I think the elf-abet blocks were talking about me. I'm an orphan."

Swish flew from her matchbox bed to settle on Carol's pillow, "Swish, kiss," she said softly.

Carol continued, "It's probably why I don't have my own robin. I was in an orphanage with Nigel and Gordon. They have a new forever family now. I'm still waiting for mine."

Jill sat up, "I'm so sorry." She got out of bed to give Carol a hug, "If it helps, the robins are so annoying to be honest. Mine leaves little feathers on my pillow."

"Does he? I never really knew my parents. I was very young when it happened. I've no other family, so had to live by my wits. That's why I'm good at sensing things. I think it's called *intuition*, though Gordon says 'I'm just good at guessing'."

"Oh," said Jill, "I'm sorry, I'm getting cold." She leapt back into her bed.

"When are you going to give Aphrodite her card?" asked Carol.

"At the 'Sad Goodbye', I saw it on Aphrodite's Big Day list. I've a feeling it's not far away. We'll know it's happening when she takes our pictures."

"Is it because of what you saw in her bedroom? What else did you see in there?"

"You promise not to tell the others?" whispered Jill.

"I promise."

"I saw lots of old photo albums and 'Thank You' cards. We're not the first children to have this dream about Christmas and I doubt we'll be the last. The thing is Aphrodite has helped every single one of them. That's why I made her a card."

"But why don't you want to tell Edward?"

"It's spooky and I don't want to frighten him. I want to be certain that we are dreaming. I'm worried if I tell Edward about the children in the pictures he might get scared and say that thing about Santa again."

"You're a good sister. This dream feels very real, doesn't it? I have another secret too and it's a big one. Promise me you won't tell?" said Carol.

"I promise."

"I know what happened to Nigel, because I was there. Nigel and Gordon were climbing a big oak tree in the orphanage garden. They kept climbing higher, but I sensed something awful was going to happen. I tried to warn them, but they wouldn't listen to me. A branch snapped. Gordon held out his hand. Nigel tried to grab it, but couldn't. Nigel hasn't walked since and Gordon blames himself."

"That's really sad," said Jill.

"Also, it happened on Christmas Day. Gordon hasn't said it, but I know he still feels so guilty. I can see it in his eyes. The doctors did all sorts of tests on Nigel. They say he'll probably never walk again, but there's still a chance. He's hoping for a miracle."

"Thank you for telling me that," said Jill. "I'll keep it a secret. I promise."

DOOR TEN

In the morning, when the children came down to breakfast they were completely unaware of the unfortunate events that had taken place in the cottage during the night. They happily enjoyed waffles, scrambled egg on toast, freshly sliced pineapple and melon. It was all very tasty, but they were about to get a really nasty shock. It began when Jill asked, "Where's Alf? Elves need their breakfast too, don't they?"

"I'll go 'n fetch Santa's little helper," said Gordon boldly.

"He's a cute little guy, no bother at all, even if the blocks said so," said Carol.

"Let's hope so," replied Jill, "Because you never can tell with elves."

"*Really*, who says?" asked Edward, with Teddy on his lap.

"I read it once, in a book," she said gulping down some orange juice.

"Where's Gordon? He's taking his time," she added, then got up and went into the lounge, calling, "Gordon... Gordon... *what's this*?" she shrieked.

She found Gordon crouched near Archie. The jack-in-the-box was open with the mince pie beside it and some crumbs scattered close by. Jack looked frightened, "Oh Jill, something truly dreadful has happened. Someone's taken some bites out of the mince pie... and look at Archie... three new doors have been opened. Its sabotage I tell you! *Sabotage*!"

Jill shrieked, "This could be the worst day *ever*!"

"I'm afraid doors 15, 19 and 22 are open and the gifts are gone," said Gordon glumly.

"The gifts... stolen? This is *definitely* the worst day ever!" she cried, "Edward, Carol, Nigel... get in here quickly... something terrible has happened."

Edward left Teddy on his chair and ran into the lounge with the others. Jill blurted out, "Someone's opened three new doors... and they've eaten some of the mince pie too."

Jack had a frightened emoji face."I did what I could," he said. "But it was dark. I felt my lid pop. Something grabbed the pie. If it wasn't for my wonky spring, well, I'd have let them have it I can tell you," he said, making a fist with his hand.

"I despair," replied Edward ironically.

"Quickly now, let's see what gifts they took," urged Jill, as she carefully picked up the mince pie.

They crowded around Archie. Kat was crouched on the mantelpiece over the fire looking down on them all. She seemed unsettled.

"Door fifteen has a picture of a Christmas pudding," said Edward.

"There's a letter to Santa on number nineteen," added Jill.

"And there's Santa's sack on door twenty-two," said Carol.

"Good elf or bad? You never can tell with elves," mumbled Jill, adding, "Where *is* that elf? I knew it... I just knew it. I wondered if we could trust him and now he's ruined Christmas. It'll probably be cancelled forever."

Edward had a thought, "But if the game is lost, shouldn't we all wake up now? Well shouldn't we?" He pinched himself, but the adventure continued.

Jack put everyone right, "May I remind you that under rule two of Archie's Advent Adventure *you* must open the doors sequentially... that is in the right order... and on the right dates. The rule only applies to the game's players... you and Edward. If, as you all suspect, Alf did it, then the game is still there to be won. It's simple really... you just need to recover the lost pieces."

"'*Simple*', he says?" said Edward, shaking his head.

"Oh Jack, that's such a relief... I do love you sometimes!" said Jill. She gave him a big soggy kiss. Jack spluttered and wobbled, "Oh, stop it now, oh and you need to keep opening Archie's other doors on the right days."

"I thought we were done for," said Gordon, picking up the mince pie crumbs.

"Put them back in my box... and NOT in your mouth," said Jack fiercely. "We're in enough trouble as it is."

He did as Jack asked, whilst Jill gave the pie back to him. "I still believe in you," she told him, but Edward shook his head.

"I know, let's open door ten!" said Carol, "I've a feeling it'll help us find Alf."

"No, not yet. I'll roll the elf-abet blocks first. They might give us a clue," said Jill. She grabbed then tumbled the blocks. Much to everyone's surprise they spelt, 'G, R, U, M, P, S'.

"Grumps?" said Carol, "Ah, it's all beginning to make sense."

"Grumps?" grumbled Jack, "Exactly, perhaps Alf isn't the culprit after all."

Kat flapped her ears, jumped down from the mantelpiece and ran off in to the kitchen.

"Here, you try Edward," urged Jill. Edward re-rolled the elf-abet blocks. They spelt, 'P, I, C, N, I, C.'

"Picnic! I don't understand. What does that mean?" he asked, looking at the others for any ideas.

Jack replied, "Edward, a picnic is when a packed meal is eaten outside."

"I know what a picnic is! Really, these bricks are all gobbledygook."

"They're nothing of the sort. The elf-abet blocks are wise. Ah, I do love a nice picnic... tuppeny rice and treacle would be just perfect," said Jack.

Edward teased Jack, "Rice and treacle? *Yuk*! The blocks are just confusing us. I bet that elf did it! We're wasting time. We need to find him before he causes any more trouble."

"Wait. Whatever's hidden behind door ten might help us," said Jill. She opened it quickly. Inside was a teddy bear with a broken ear. "Edward, you really need to see this," she said curiously. However, as she took it out the miniature bear simply vanished.

Edward and the others missed the moment. They had been distracted by unexpected voices in the kitchen. There they found Edward's bear enjoying tea with Alf and Swish, with Kat on the table happily licking cream from a scone.

It was the most unlikely of sights especially as Teddy had doubled in size. They were making a terrible mess too with bits of scone and cookies scattered about and a bottle knocked over. Milk had poured from it and made a puddle on the kitchen floor.

"Ah, there you are Edward. I'm having a teddy bear's picnic. Tea anyone?" asked Teddy in a surprisingly gruff voice.

"*Teddy*?" whispered Edward, "You're really real... and big!"

"I'm sorry. I can't hear you. You'll need to speak up as I'm a bit deaf in one ear."

Edward spoke louder, "I said, 'You're real'." Overjoyed, he tried to cuddle his teddy.

"Yes I'm real," he replied slowly and coldly. "Whoa! Okay, that's enough. You can stop now. Don't squeeze too tight. And that tickles," he said, brushing Edward off.

"Edward, your teddy's stuffed. He couldn't eat another thing!" claimed Alf, laughing at his own joke.

"Ha, ha!" said Edward sarcastically. "Tell me elf, why did you do it and where are the gifts?" he asked with a cold hard stare.

"My name is Alf, not Elf," he replied casually, "Hey, don't look at me like that. What did I do?"

"You know what you did. Where's the letter to Santa, the Christmas pudding and Santa's sack of presents? Hand them over." Edward put his hands out and waited.

"Why would I do that, I don't much like Christmas pudding?" said Alf, adjusting his hat. "Relax Edward. Be happy. This is your teddy bear's picnic." He picked up a teapot, "More tea Teddy?"

"Why thank you kind Sir," replied Teddy, trying his best to balance a cup between his paws.

"I'm sorry, but this is no time for a picnic," said Jill.

Teddy turned his head to look at Jill, "Oh you're sorry are you?" he snorted. "No time for a picnic you say... well don't worry Jill, now let's be clear, you're not invited. I prefer to dine with my friends."

Swish seemed happy enough with that. "Teddy, picnic, tea, friends," she said softly.

"But *I'm* your best friend Teddy, not them," claimed Edward. "Don't worry. We'll go on that picnic real soon. I promise." He grabbed Teddy by a paw.

"Hey. What are you doing? You can't carry me about anymore. I'm real... and big... and I don't like being picked up now."

"But Teddy?" said Edward sadly.

"You heard him," said Alf, "He's all grown up now, and so should you be."

Edward's eyes filled with tears. He left the toys alone and returned to the lounge. He sat in Aphrodite's chair, sighed and whispered to his robin, "That's just what my father said I should do."

***

When Aphrodite came home she threw her coat on the floor as usual, but this time the clumpy boots stayed on. She had a very keen eye for Archie's Advent calendar doors and knew the second she saw him that something very dramatic and very serious had happened.

"*Astonishing*! I shall have to fetch my camera," she announced.

"Your camera, and so soon?" said Jill. "Look at us Aphrodite. None of us are smiling."

"Well children you should be for everything's perfectly wonderful."

Edward was very confused, "How can it be wonderful? Someone's stolen Santa's letter, his sack and the Christmas pudding... and worst of all Teddy doesn't need me anymore."

"Not only that, we haven't written our letters to Santa yet!" said Jill, "So it's all going horribly wrong. It's a catastrophe."

Kat sniffed at Archie and hissed.

"On the contrary, it's wonderful children because Archie's Advent Adventure is no picnic. To win you'll need courage, skill, brains... and an enormous slice of good fortune. Trust me, it could have been *so* much worse," she said joyfully.

Jill whispered to herself, "Maybe I am mistaken. She's far too happy for a sad goodbye."

"But the gifts were taken," said Edward. "And we think it might be Alf. That elf was on that shelf last night. It has to be *him*," he added pointing to the elf who was back on that shelf, with Swish right beside him.

"Does it now? And have you tried looking in my bedroom for the lost gifts?" asked Aphrodite.

Jill replied, "Eh, the sign on the door reads 'No Children Allowed'."

"Yes it does, doesn't it?" said Aphrodite, rolling her tongue in her mouth. "But it doesn't say no elves or fairies though, does it? And look at those two sitting together. They seem to be getting along just fine." So she sung, "Swish and the elf, sitting on the shelf, 'K, I, S, S, I, N, G!'"

"Triple yuk!" blurted Edward.

Jack cleared his throat, "Erm, Aphrodite, I'm afraid to say the elf-abet blocks spelt 'grumps'."

"Hmm... I thought as much," she said with a troubled look, "But I'm sure I bolted the front door last night! We can't be too careful, especially in this house."

"So, do you think the missing gifts could be in your room then?" asked Jill hopefully.

"I very much doubt it Jill, there's barely enough room to swing a... no I best not say it. Let's not worry about that now. I'll go and fetch my camera."

Aphrodite did just that. She clicked her fingers which lit another 'Smiling Happy Faces' candle and took plenty of memorable photos for her album.

However, the truth was that Jill's feared 'sad goodbye' was rapidly approaching. It was why Aphrodite invited all the children to write their letters to Santa. Edward played along, but refused to tell Jill what he'd written, so she did the same to him. They gave their letters to Aphrodite. She addressed them to Santa Claus, The Workshop, Tinsel Town, Santarctica, North Pole.

"But how will they reach him? You don't get any mail here, do you?" asked Jill.

"Worry not children. The cottage always finds a way."

DOOR ELEVEN

It was all becoming very crowded around the kitchen table, but Conjuring Cottage didn't disappoint. On day eleven it served up a feast fit for fairy tales. Teddy ended up with sticky paws covered in honey and Alf had a dollop of strawberry jam on his nose. He tried to lick it off with his tongue, but failed. Edward, though, distracted everyone by tugging on the curly white hair on his chin. He stretched it out and found it now reached all the way to his belly button.

"I really don't like the look of that, not one bit," said Alf.

"Be quiet Alf. Don't you belong on a shelf?" replied Edward sharply.

"Hey buddy. Quit being a meanie."

Teddy had something to say about that, "Jill put me on the top shelf once, out of Edward's reach. Do you remember?"

"There was a good reason for that *wasn't* there Edward? You broke Jack's spring, didn't you?" replied Jill.

"I told you before. It was an accident."

"And that's why you almost pulled my ear off, wasn't it Jill?" sniped Teddy.

"I'm very sorry Teddy. I was upset about Jack."

This was all news to Edward, "So you did do it! I said it was you and you lied. And that was a bad lie, not a pretend one." He slapped his toast down. Some marmalade splashed up and hit Teddy on the nose. He happily licked it clean.

"I'm sorry Edward," said Jill sadly.

"I think we should light one of Aphrodite's 'Smiling Happy Faces' candles," chirped Carol.

***

When everybody went into the lounge, Jack was already out of his box. He had a disappointed face, "I heard everything. Now you say it was an accident? But I remember everything clearly, like it was yesterday." He was looking right at Edward sitting uneasily in Aphrodite's chair. Teddy was sat beside him.

"You scared me when you popped up. I was only three years old. I didn't mean to hit you. I didn't mean to break your spring. I'm sorry Jack," said Edward.

"You're sorry? When someone turns my crank and my music plays, I just have to pop. I didn't mean to scare you Edward."

"Jack, when I have my picnic, you're very welcome to come," said Teddy, "I'll make sure there's plenty of treacle... nice and sticky!"

Alf teased them, "Oh for goodness sake. 'I love you, no I love you more'. I can't be doing with all this gooey nonsense. Can you just open the next door Edward, please?"

Edward did as Alf requested. He got off the armchair and opened door eleven. He took out a brightly decorated Christmas cracker in red and gold with a Christmas tree sticker on it.

"Oh, it's a cracker. What shall we do with it?" asked Edward as it grew bigger.

"Why pull it off course!" said Jack, "There's nothing in the rules to forbid it."

Jill wasn't Edward's favourite person right now, so he chose Carol, "Carol do you want to pull it with me?"

"Edward, I'm allowed, am I?" she asked, fluttering her eyelashes.

Jack was tapping his box and thinking, "I'm double-checking the rules in my head... No, I think you're fine. Edward can pull his cracker with any piece he likes."

Jill was most displeased, "Edward how could you? I'm your sister," she said, but he didn't reply. *"Fine!* I know what you're doing, you chose her because she's pretty didn't you? Oh do what you like. I'm not watching." She stormed off upstairs in a grump. Kat didn't follow, but Swish did, which was wise given her fear of loud noises.

"Grab the end and pull hard!" said Edward.

Edward and Carol stood right in the middle of the room and tugged hard on the cracker. Everyone waited nervously for the bang. The robins tucked their heads deep into their feathers and Alf leapt up onto his shelf and covered his ears. Teddy did the same with his good ear. Yet when the cracker split, there was no bang! Carol was left holding the bigger end with the tree sticker on it.

"What's inside?" asked Edward.

Carol looked inside the cracker. First out was a glittery gold paper hat, which she unfolded.

"It's a paper crown," she said.

"You won it. Put it on," suggested Edward. She did so. It settled nicely on her ringlets. She fluttered her eyelashes and smiled warmly.

"Cracking," joked Edward. "Is there anything else?"

She reached inside the cracker again and found a small strip of paper.

"I think it's a riddle. I'll read it, 'What do you call two robins in love?'" She waited to see if anyone had an answer, then said, "Tweet hearts!" Everyone groaned, but the robins chirped merrily and fluffed out their red breasts in triumph.

"Anything more?" asked Nigel.

"I'll see," she said and dug her fingers deeper into the cracker. "Wait... here it is, the main prize." She took out a tightly rolled piece of glossy paper and began to open it up, "It looks like a map... it is a map... how curious."

"Where, let me see," asked Edward. They held the map together, pointing eagerly at some of the places on it, "Oh my... look here it says, Conjuring Cottage and there Tinsel Town."

Jill marched down the stairs. "*Let me see that*," she huffed. In fact, they all gathered about the map.

Alf hopped up on to Rocky's head to look, "Oh it's just a map of the Kingdom of Santarctica! I know all these places, Dash Away, No Turning Back, and Candy Cane Forest. Oh, and there's, Bah Humbug."

"Bah Humbug, what's that?" asked Edward.

"You've not heard of Bah Humbug?" said Alf surprised, "Why it's a fortress."

"A fortress?" said Jill doubtfully.

Jack made an important decision. He looked at Alf and said, “I think we should tell them. They need to find out soon enough, and Aphrodite did say their real adventure is only just beginning.”

Alf nodded, took a deep breath, then blurted out, "Bah Humbug is where the grumps live."

"So that's where they are," said Carol knowingly.

"The grumps, what exactly are they?" asked Edward.

Jack took a deep breath then said, "The Christmas Grumps. They don't like Christmas, not one bit and want to end it forever. They're short, mean, ugly and green. They have tiny ears and huge noses with a tremendous sense of smell. They have no teeth, so live on cold soggy sprouts. They're so miserable their down-turned mouths droop so low their chins would almost reach the ground if not for their pot-bellies. And they waddle around on stumpy little legs."

"They sound ghastly," uttered Nigel.

Jack continued, "Grumps can't sleep at night, so that's when you'll usually spot them. They have glowing orange eyes that can see in the dark and by day they prefer to hide in places where the sun never shines."

"Glowing orange eyes?" asked Edward.

"And I can tell you, they most certainly do not like elves," insisted Alf.

"Grumps bad. Bad grumps," said Swish.

Jack glanced at Edward, "Oh I almost forgot. Every grump also has a single silvery-white curly hair growing out of their chin."

Everyone gasped in horror and turned to stare at Edward. Shaken, he cried, "... NO! It's not what you're thinking. I'm not one of them. I'm *not* a grump."

***

When Aphrodite came home she had no time to remove her coat, let alone her boots, before the children swamped her.

Jill spoke first, "Aphrodite, thank goodness. Jack and Alf told us all about the grumps."

"Perfect," she replied with a big smile.

"And we got a Christmas cracker from Archie today... with a map inside it," added Edward with his hands still on it, "Look."

"Better than perfect."

"It's a map of Santarctica, with Conjuring Cottage and Tinsel Town on it," said Carol.

"And places called, Quietly Does It and A Long Way Down," added Nigel, twiddling with his bow tie.

Then Gordon said, "But the worst of it is Bah Humbug, where the grumps live. That sounds a terrible and scary place."

"Sadly, though," said Teddy. "There's no mention of a place to picnic. What kind of a map does that? It's quite useless."

"How stupendous!" cried Aphrodite, "Now children, bear, please I must throw off my coat and boots. There's much to do."

The children stood aside. She took off her coat and threw it. Unfortunately for Alf it landed right on top of him. Teddy tried to come to his rescue but his hands were still very sticky with honey. It made Aphrodite's shaggy brown coat less fashionable than ever. Not that she seemed concerned. She threw away her sunglasses, pulled her laces and kicked off her boots. One landed wrong side up on Rocky's tail, where Swish happened to be sitting. The other just missed Kat, but landed upside down on top of Jack, just as he had popped up from his box. It was most unfortunate for the Smelly Wellie candles were lit.

"Now that's bootylicious!" claimed Aphrodite.

Everyone was unharmed, so the children giggled.

DOOR TWELVE

Dawn was welcomed by one of Edward's booming snores that followed his forty winks. During the night Edward had woken up Nigel and Gordon. Together they'd pulled back the curtains and looked out of the window into the darkness. Once again, they saw several pairs of glowing orange eyes looking back at them from the woods. Edward pointed them out, "Look there, do you see the grumps? They stole Archie's gifts. We have to get them back. My guess is they took them to Bah Humbug. We've got the map now. We could sneak in during the day and grab them."

"They look really scary. I don't want to go anywhere near them," said Nigel.

"Me neither," agreed Gordon.

"But they're not scary at all. I don't think they'll hurt us. They just feel sad. I'm sure of it," claimed Edward. As he spoke he felt the curly hair on his chin tingle.

***

At breakfast Edward was doing his best to think of a plan to recover Archie's stolen gifts. He studied the map of Santarctica, busily twiddling the pesky hair on his chin. He had a look about him that Jill hadn't seen before - it was determination. In fact, Edward was so determined he finally succeeded in clicking his fingers.

"There I did it! I must be really growing up!" he claimed excitedly.

"Practice makes perfect," said Carol, still wearing her paper crown.

Edward clicked his fingers again, as if issuing a command, "Can we hurry up please Jill? I really want to see what's behind door twelve."

"Edward, please don't click your fingers at me," complained Jill, "And what happened to, *'I hate Christmas'*?"

"I never said that."

"Oh yes you did."

"Oh no I didn't. I told you before. I actually said I don't like it! Anyway, I'm fighting it Jill, that's what's happened. Daddy said I need to grow up fast, so I am. And the elf-abet blocks read, 'Father', didn't they. I want us to win this game for him," he said.

"Well that's more like it," replied his sister.

Edward was feeling rather proud of himself. He looked at Carol. "You're still wearing your paper hat," he said happily.

"I know. It's stuck fast. I had to sleep in it last night."

"My breakfast is stuck fast. It's very sticky," said Teddy. He had peanut butter stuck to the ends of his paws.

"It is when you have paws for a knife and fork Teddy," said Jill. She was obviously trying to make it up with the bear.

Teddy licked his paws, "Paw tatty Teddy. Yummy!"

Alf laughed, causing his pointy hat to fall into his porridge. Splat!

***

Jill was free of all stickiness when she tugged at door twelve. Inside something glistened. It was a delicate crystal snowflake decoration. She took it out very carefully and held it in her open palm. The beautiful snowflake sparkled with all the colours of the rainbow. Jack had been watching, "Let it snow!" he announced, and with a sparkle and a flash the snowflake vanished from Jill's hand.

"Look, it's snowing," cried Carol.

Everyone hurried to look out of the window. Giant snowflakes were falling. Some were almost the size of their hands.

The excited children slipped on their boots and dashed outside. Everyone that was, but Edward. He and Jack were alone, with Kat.

Jack tapped on his box. He spoke with an angry emoji face, “Eh-um... don’t tell me you hate snow too now Edward? Most children love snow... almost as much as Christmas. Why don’t you go outside and have some fun... with the others?”

“I’ve little time for fun. Snow is the last thing we need right now. We must get the stolen gifts back and I’ve a good idea where they are.” He picked up the elf-abet blocks and rolled them.

They spelt, H, U, M, B, U, G. “There. I knew it,” he said triumphantly.

"Quite Edward. Your task is to reach Tinsel Town by Christmas Day and arrive there with all of Archie's doors opened on the right days and with all the gifts in place, unless of course you actually *do* want Christmas cancelled forever. Is that what you want?"

"No, of course I don't want that," he said frowning.

"So you say. Edward, I'm glad we're alone at last. I've been waiting for this moment. You might be pretending, like you did when your sister opened door one. You heard everything I said, didn't you?"

"That's not true!"

"You hate Christmas, just like a grump. You don't believe in Santa, just like a grump. You have that curly white hair on your chin, just like a grump. You can't sleep at night, just like a grump. And now you don't want to have fun, just like a grump. Perhaps you undid the bolt on the front door so the grumps could come in? Was it you Edward?" asked Jack menacingly.

"Shut up! Get back in that box or I'll break your spring for good," snapped Edward.

"So you're mean too now, just like a grump. Maybe one day you'll be the King of the Grumps!"

Kat flapped her ears.

"Think what you like box boy. Watch me. I'm going outside to have fun, right now! I'm going to make snowballs," said Edward. He grabbed his coat and boots.

"There's nothing worse than a grump with the hump! And there'll be an army of grumps waiting for you at Bah Humbug led by General Grump. You definitely don't want to mess with him."

Edward stomped back over to Jack, "I don't care how many grumps there are. I'm not afraid of grumps. I feel sorry for them."

"And now you like them. That's the real reason you want to go there, isn't it Edward? It's got nothing to do with the lost gifts."

"If anyone's pretending it's you Jack. You got the rules wrong on purpose, didn't you? And you didn't tell us how to win this game either, until now. I had to work that out for myself. If you ask me, I'd say you want us to lose."

"That's all very unfair. I have a wonky spring, *remember*?" He pulled the lid down on his box.

***

Kat didn't much like snow. She sat on the window ledge and looked outside. The snow was falling thick and fast. It settled quickly, turning Santarctica into a winter wonderland. The children ran about excitedly. Teddy was having a glorious time. He followed his own footsteps, rolled about and tried catching snowflakes on his tongue. Nigel rode Rocky. He was perfectly at home in the snow, using his curved wooden rockers as skis. It wasn't long before a snowball fight began. Alf threw the first one, "Take that Buddy," he cried as it hit Edward on the back of the head. He threw another. It splattered into Gordon's tummy. Soon snowballs were flying every which way. Swish and the robins took cover on the chimney.

Aphrodite was rather fond of a snowball fight too and was a humdinger of a shot. At the first sight of snow, she rushed home and ambushed the children in the garden. Her first snowball struck Teddy on the bottom. Her second hit Jill on the arm.

Aphrodite was about to throw a third when everyone turned to aim at her. One snowball knocked her sunglasses off, the next two landed in the last of her antler hair and the rest stuck to her sticky shaggy coat.

"My lumps, my lumps, my lovely snowball lumps," sang Aphrodite, before bringing the snowball fight to an abrupt end, "Enough merrymaking children, for there's much to do. Delicious beverages await... there are mugs of hot chocolate and freshly baked shortbread on the table. Quickly now before..."

But Jill interrupted her, "The Christmas grumps grab you."

Aphrodite chuckled, “Oh, and I almost forgot. Come back Peter, come back Paul.” She twiddled her thumbs to call the children’s robins down from the rooftop and went inside, leaving her sunglasses lying in the snow.

***

As the other children finished off their shortbread and hot chocolate, Edward followed Aphrodite into the kitchen and asked her a very important question, “Aphrodite, where do grumps come from?”

“Splendid question Edward. Legend has it that the grown-ups are to blame. Every time an adult moans about Christmas a new grump appears. The more they complain the meaner the grumps become. And when the grumps grumble, the fortress at Bah Humbug gets bigger. It is said that the fortress is *alive*, but Edward, Christmas wouldn’t be Christmas without the grumps.”

“Is that because Christmas can be a painful time for some grown-ups?” asked Edward.

“Yes, and some children too, we mustn’t forget that. It’s why you’re here Edward and why you can’t sleep at night without your forty winks, but it’s a talent that might come in handy... very handy.”

“But what happens when eh... children moan about Christmas?”

“Oh Edward, let’s just say that there’s usually a very good reason for that. A very good one indeed,” replied Aphrodite, trying to tidy Edward’s hair a little with her fingers.

***

Ever since their arrival at Conjuring Cottage the children had enjoyed delicious slap-up meals. So, as the snow continued to fall, they were most surprised to find the kitchen table was laid with a box of chocolates, a tin of biscuits and a bag of sweets.

“Dinner is served,” said Aphrodite in all seriousness.

“This is ridiculous. Aphrodite we can’t possibly have these for dinner,” Jill said.

“But what about our teeth, you always said we have to look after them?” asked Edward.

“Ah, but these are no ordinary chocolates, biscuits and sweets. They’re sugar free and won’t harm your precious pearly whites at all. Here, just look at the selection menu for the chocolates,” urged Aphrodite.

Jill was goggle-eyed, "Vegetable lasagne, pepperoni pizza, spaghetti bolognaise, fish and chips!"

Gordon licked his lips as Edward read out some more flavours, "Sweet and sour chicken with rice, sausages and mash, cheese on toast... but no sprouts?"

"Absolutely *no* sprouts... that's another precaution," said Aphrodite. "Now, one sweet and one biscuit will fill you up good and proper. Trust me you won't be hungry again 'til morning. Not that you need worry any more Edward. Keep eating the way you are and any day soon you'll have a little round belly that shakes like jelly when you laugh, just like Santa," which amused Gordon greatly.

Edward, though, stood up straight and held his tummy in. He shook his head and mumbled, "I think Aphrodite needs glasses."

"Now, let's look at the biscuits," said Aphrodite.

Carol read the menu on the tin's lid, "Apple pie and cream, jam roly-poly, spotted-dick and custard, cheesecake, and trifle."

"There's a packet of Goody Goody Gumdrops too... in some very tempting flavours... strawberry milkshake, milky tea, lemonade and more. Just like drinking the real thing! Now tuck in everybody. Bon appétit!"

Aphrodite was right. One of each was more than plenty, even for Gordon. "Mmm... you should try the fish and chips... they're so yummy!" he said.

As they chewed on their meal Aphrodite told them, “Children, you’ll need the chocolate, biscuits and sweets for the rest of your adventure and some scented candles too.”

“Scented candles?” asked Jill, with a mouthful of biscuit.

“Yes... scented candles, Soggy Sprout Farts, Smiling Happy Faces and Gooey Ear Wax in fact. And remember, one finger click for on and two clicks for off! Oh and some jars of my marvellously gloopy green beauty mask. It’s everlasting and will do wonders for your complexion. Just look at me!” Aphrodite suggested, smiling widely.

“All sticky, smelly and green,” said Teddy, licking the chocolate from his paws.

DOOR THIRTEEN

The children enjoyed another fabulous breakfast. Teddy had boiled egg and toastie soldiers, but found it tricky dipping them into his runny egg. It was a very messy affair and the egg went everywhere. Teddy playfully patted Kat with icky-eggy paws. She was too busy cleaning herself to notice, until Teddy got some egg up his nose and sneezed. It splattered all over Kat. She leapt from the table and scampered into the lounge.

Kat found Aphrodite sitting in her favourite chair wiping her nose. "I've got the sniffles today Kat. It was probably the snowball fight that did it. I hope it doesn't spoil my singing," she said. Kat leapt up on to her lap, purring and rubbing herself against Aphrodite. The icky-eggy mess stuck to her handkerchief, but Aphrodite didn't notice and wiped her nose again. Poor Aphrodite!

After breakfast, the children were extremely surprised to find Aphrodite sat in her armchair. She had been waiting for them.

"There you are. We're just going to...," said Jill.

"Open door thirteen," confirmed Aphrodite. "It's unlucky for some, me mostly!"

"What's wrong with your nose?" Edward asked.

"I'm all sniffles today!" she replied, then blew her nose LOUDLY. Her nose was now an icky-eggy mess.

"But it's yellow!" Carol said boldly.

"Is it?" She looked in her handkerchief. "No, it looks green to me!" she said, and showed the children.

"Four times *Yuk*!" cried Edward.

The children giggled. Jack came out of his box to see what all the fuss was about. He had a happy face with tears. "Mmm... what eggs-actly is going on here?" he asked.

"I got icky with my eggy," murmured Teddy.

Swish swished by, "Icky, eggy, Kat, nose, yellow."

Aphrodite rubbed her nose then looked at her finger tips, "Kat, hanky, nose, yellow! I have egg on my face. Children I must apologise once more for my appearance. Door thirteen if you please?"

It was Edward's turn to open one of Archie's doors. He knelt down in front of it. For the first time since he arrived at the cottage Edward was wearing a Christmas jumper. It had a picture of a Christmas teddy on it. In fact, every child was wearing one, which delighted Aphrodite. Jill's jumper had a robin on it, Carol's a penguin, Nigel's a reindeer and Gordon's had a mince pie. Alf celebrated by jumping about excitedly.

"Oooh my, just look at all the wonderful jumpers. What merriment!" chuckled Aphrodite, licking the egg from her fingertips.

Edward gave a little smile and opened door thirteen. Inside he found a small wooden sleigh. He took it out and showed everyone. In a sparkle and a flash it vanished.

"Quickly... outside children!" requested Aphrodite.

They grabbed their coats and boots and opened the front door. The snow had stopped but lay thick and crunchy. Just beyond the picket fence was a majestic red and gold sleigh with room enough for all of them.

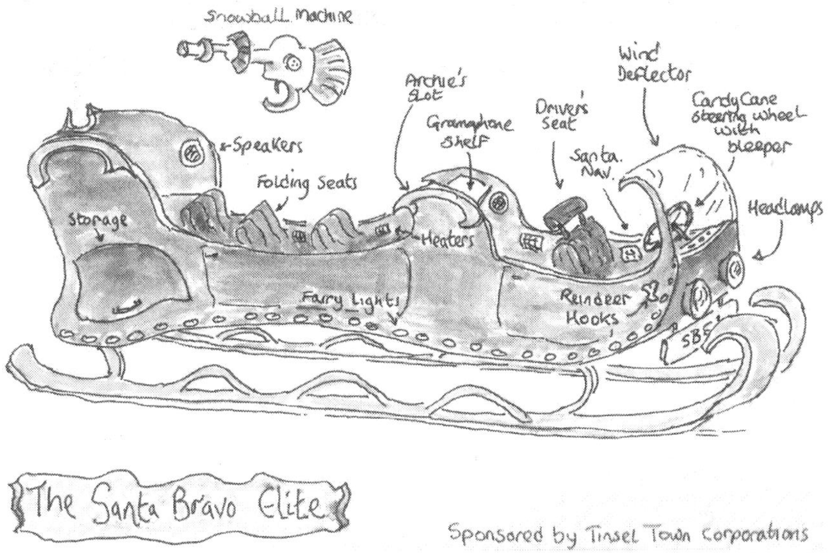

"WOW," shrieked Alf, "It's the super silent deluxe model, the Santa Bravo Elite."

Aphrodite was delighted, "Sensational isn't it? Sponsored by Tinsel Town corporations, it has Santa-lite navigation, flashing fairy lights in red, gold and green, heaters and surround sound speakers. It even has a portable snowball making machine! Step aboard children, get yourself acquainted."

Edward sat at the controls. The sleigh had a candy-striped steering wheel with a red centre that glowed when it was time to open Archie's next door. There were also Stop and Go pedals, a headlights switch and a shelf for the gramophone. "Does it fly?" Edward asked.

"Don't be silly, you'll need Santa's reindeers for that," said Alf laughing.

"So how does it move?" asked Jill.

"That's easy-peasy too. We'll use rocking Rocky! At full speed he has the power of twenty horses. Come now children, let's rein him up and get everything loaded on," urged Aphrodite.

At the back of the sleigh was a place to store all they needed for their journey. Beneath it was ample space for Christmas jumpers' aplenty, scented candles, jars of gloopy green face mask, chocolate box selections, tins of biscuits, sweets, and for good luck, Aphrodite put in a bag of Clementine oranges. Aphrodite also brought out the wind-up gramophone, put it on the shelf and plugged it in. She also found a spot for Nigel's old wheelchair – just in case, but Nigel turned his nose up at it. He much preferred riding Rocky now.

"Is Archie coming with us too?" asked Jill.

"Absolutely, and every single gift that came out of his doors, including the elf-abet blocks, the jack-in-the-box... Swish and Teddy. I'll fetch Archie. He's heavy! We mustn't break him."

Jill dashed back to the cottage, almost tripping over Kat who was sat on the doorstep licking the last of the icky-eggy from her fur. She picked up Jack's box, closed his lid and turned his crank handle. 'Pop Goes the Weasel' played and on the pop he crawled back out with love hearts for eyes. "Thank you Jill," said Jack. "I enjoyed that. I am truly loved and so looking forward to our adventure."

Jill followed Aphrodite back to the sleigh. As she did so, Edward gave Jack a long hard stare. He remembered their recent argument and thought about the torn ear of his bear.

"Where is Teddy?" Edward asked.

Paw prints were nearby in the snow. Teddy was singing, "Round and round the garden, like a Teddy Bear. One step, two steps..." Edward trooped through the snow and grabbed him, "Tickly under there!" And this time, Teddy didn't make a fuss.

Aphrodite carefully placed Archie in the sleigh, making sure it was safe and secure, and kissed the star at the top of the tree, "Okay, Archie should be fine there. Promise me you'll take extra care of him. I don't want him broken. Come now children, make haste. We must make the most of the daylight. Oh, and there's a special place under the steering wheel to keep the map of Santarctica. Whatever you do, don't lose it."

Jill was feeling emotional, "So it's *really* happening?" She whispered, "The sad goodbye?"

"But where shall we sleep?" asked Edward.

"Sleep? Oh, that reminds me? You'll need your jim-jams, dressing gowns and slippers... and your toothbrushes too. You must look after your smile."

So they all dashed back inside to collect them. As they returned Nigel said, "I'm afraid. What about the grumps, won't they grab us? I want to ride Rocky, but only if it's safe."

"Exactly! Those grumps give me goosebumps," said Gordon. "And won't we get cold. I like a nice snugly bed."

"Worry not children, I promise you won't feel the cold much... and the grumps cannot harm you," claimed Aphrodite, busily double-checking the items on the sleigh.

"It's under Santa clause six," said Alf as he hopped about excitedly.

Aphrodite nodded, "A Santa clause? Santa Claus' Santa clauses. A sixth clause for Santa. Oh my goodness how terribly confusing," she admitted.

"Hold your horses," said Jack, "I'm the legal expert. If anyone explains such things it's me, understood?" He tapped his box. "Yes, I remember now, it's rule six! It states clearly that grumps shouldn't hurt children!"

"Ah so that was rule six then, was it?" said Jill.

"Stupendous! Right children, have we got everything?"

"No! We still don't have the Santa Sweet, do we Edward? You lost it, didn't you?" said Jill in frustration.

"So it's *still* missing!" said Jack, shaking his head.

"Yes, it's still missing, but I already explained that. I didn't lose it. I just don't remember where I put it."

"How very convenient," grumbled Jack.

"Don't worry Edward, I'm sure you'll remember soon," said Carol reassuringly to Edward.

"Now, now, squabble not! It's all splendiferous. Listen very carefully children. The sweetest things can appear when you least expect them to... Right, go grab your coats, hats and gloves."

Once the children did so, Aphrodite said, "The first stop will be No Turning Back. Enter that into the *Santa. Nav.*"

Jill volunteered to do it, "Right, I'm the eldest. I'll do it... and I'll drive."

"That's irrelevant," said Jack, "Rule seven says that the elf-abet blocks must choose who drives the Santa Bravo Elite."

"Another rule? *Fine*!" said Jill. She collected the blocks and rolled them over the snow. They spelt, '-, D, W, A, R, D'. "That's *so* unfair... and he gets car sick. I've seen him almost turn green. Besides, I only have four letters in my name. It's ridiculous. It was never going to be me. So why should he drive?" huffed Jill.

"Let's find out then, shall we?" said Edward as he rolled the blocks. They spelt, 'W, I, N, K, -, R'.

"Winker?" asked Jill, confused.

"Pardon me?" asked Teddy winking.

"That's it! Edward's a winker, because of his forty winks," said Carol happily.

Edward understood, "It's true. I can stay awake, drive at night and keep a look out." He started winking and counting to remind everyone of his superpowers.

"*Fine*! You drive then," said Jill.

"Don't worry, I will!"

"Dear me, you two are still bickering. Christmas should be a time for peace and love and you have to all work as a team," said Aphrodite, as she headed back to the cottage.

Jill and Edward understood and apologised to each other, though, for revenge, Jill poked her tongue out at Edward when she was sure nobody was watching.

Aphrodite returned cradling Kat, "I knew there was a little something I'd forgotten," she mumbled, "Kat wants to see you off too, don't you Kat."

Kat meowed and blinked her golden eyes.

"But Aphrodite, aren't you coming too?" asked Edward.

"Oh no, the sleigh's fully loaded already... and besides Kat doesn't like the snow. Remember, this is your game and your adventure children, whereas I have much to do. I must finish the plans for my big day."

"But... will we see you again?" asked Edward.

"And the cottage, will we be coming back?" added Jill.

"Perhaps, it depends on how well you play... remember children, courage, skill, teamwork, passion... these things will win the day... so let's have no tears. I can't be doing with tears," she said with watery eyes. "This is not a sad farewell... we're warming up for a victory parade! Now, is everyone ready, for its fun to ride on a one horse open sleigh? Let the map guide you."

All the children hugged Aphrodite in turn and kissed Kat on the top of her head. Edward was the last to climb aboard the sleigh. As he did so, he whispered to Jill something about 'Thank You' cards. They giggled.

"Whispering, sneaky! Giggling, cheeky!" said Aphrodite as she clutched at her handkerchief. To the tune of the Christmas Carol, 'We Three Kings of Orient Are' she waved and sang them off,

"Three broken springs on my wing-backed chair.
But worry not, for I do not care.
I am gorgeous, booty-licious, Aph-ro-di-te.
I'm a, thing of wonder, a beauty queen.
Prettiest lady you've ever seen.
Always smiling, most beguiling...
Guide them through their Christmas dream."

"Goodbye Conjuring Cottage, goodbye Aphrodite, goodbye Kat," cried the children, waving.

"We'll see you again soon!" said Carol, which was a promising thing indeed.

***

Aphrodite watched the sleigh until it reached the edge of the Lost Woods. When she returned to the cottage it felt empty, quiet and cold, for it lacked the warm glow the children had brought to her heart. She relit the log fire.

Eventually, when she went to bed, she noticed Kat had left a fresh scratch on her bedroom door frame. On her pillow she found five Thank You cards. One had a Christmas tree drawn on the front. The others had pictures of Santa, a cottage in the snow, a Christmas pudding and a Christmas angel. There were many kind words inside, sprinkled with, 'love'.

"What comes around goes around. How absolutely marvellously stupendously brilliant," she said.

Kat meowed in approval and curled up next to Aphrodite and fell fast asleep.

"I *do* love you Kat," said Aphrodite.

***

Meanwhile, with Nigel bravely riding on Rocky, the one horse open sleigh had long since entered the woods. It found an arrowed sign with robins perched upon it, which read, 'Dash Away'.

"Now Rocky, on Rocky. Dash away, dash away!" urged Edward loudly.

Rocky picked up speed. He dashed over the snow, weaving dramatically between countless trees. Many robins flew alongside the sleigh until it broke clear of the woods. The riders were met by an open festive landscape scattered with towering fir trees, holly bushes and oddly shaped grey rocks. It meant there were plenty of places where the sun never shone and snow never fell and that was simply perfect for Grumps.

"It's very beautiful, just how I imagined it to be," said Carol.

"And so peaceful," added Jill.

They dashed onwards for the rest of the day, passing some penguins and a pair of polar bears far-off in the distance.

Jill said, “Polar bears? We must be close to the North Pole. I hope we'll see the northern lights once the sun goes down.”

Teddy was very excited. He did his best to clap but his paws just made a strange ‘pad-pad’ sound. All the while he said, “More bears, oh goody. Are we going to stop for a picnic soon? Did we pack a blanket?”

“Don’t worry Teddy. You’ll get your picnic. I promise,” said Alf, putting an arm around Teddy.

“HANDS OFF! He’s my teddy, not yours. I'll decide when that happens and who can go on his picnic,” shouted Edward as he drove.

“Oh yes, the picnic. Blast, we didn’t pack any treacle,” muttered Jack, peeping out on the Kingdom of Santarctica through a half-open lid. As he spoke they passed an ominous sign. It read, ‘Watch Out: Grumps About.’

Carol said what she was thinking, "Aphrodite never did say where we would sleep for the night, did she? But I've a feeling we'll be fine."

"Well, whatever happens, I'm in no state to climb a tree to get away from them, I can tell you," said Nigel.

"There won't be any tree climbing Nigel, none at all," insisted Gordon.

"I'm sure there will be somewhere to stay at No Turning Back, a log cabin... something," said Carol with confidence.

Jack came further out of his box, "Shush now. Sound carries far in Santarctica. We mustn't let the grumps know we're here," he warned.

***

The sun dropped lower in the sky making the fir trees cast long shadows. There were more and more oddly shaped rocks, so plenty of places for grumps to hide. As the night took hold Rocky tired. The children were becoming sleepy. They'd each had a chocolate and a biscuit, but they were soon rubbing their eyes. Thankfully, the Santa. Nav told them their destination was close.

Everyone else was asleep when Edward saw the oddly enormous sign No Turning Back appear at last in the sleigh's headlights. Yet, alarmingly, there was no cabin to be seen! Exhausted, Rocky could barely move. He used his last ounce of strength to drag the sleigh up to the sign, but just before the sleigh came to rest Rocky's rocker ran over a hidden trip wire buried beneath the snow. Suddenly, a trail of jingle bells sprang up and RANG-OUT loudly, echoing across the kingdom, waking everyone aboard the sleigh with a start.

Jack cried, "Oh no. It's a trap. The jingle bells will jangle all the way to Bah Humbug. The grumps will know we're here now."

Jill shrieked, "This is definitely the worse day of my life by far *ever*."

Swish covered her mouth as she yawned then said, "Grumps sad. Grumps bad."

"Grumps or no grumps, I'm still not climbing any trees," said Nigel, before crying 'Rocky Off' which took him back to the seat beside Jill, which was where his wheelchair was folded.

Far away, in Bah Humbug the grumps stirred when they heard the jingle bells. In their towering fortress, they turned away from cauldrons of boiling soggy sprouts. The jingly-jangly sound made their orange eyes glow brighter than ever.

All at once the grumps chanted, “I’m happy being a grump. I’m happy having the hump. We don’t like Christmas, not one bit.”

Their words drifted across Santarctica and reached the one horse open sleigh. ‘I’m happy being a grump. I’m happy having the hump. We don’t like Christmas, not one bit.’

“It’s the grumps. We’re done for!” cried Gordon.

“Come now... they’re just a bit moody,” said Edward, who, strangely, seemed to be looking forward to meeting them. But the wonder of the northern lights dancing on the horizon was lost on the other children. Under the stars and a half-moon they huddled together for warmth and protection. Soon many pairs of glowing orange eyes began to appear in the darkness. The sound of shuffling grew louder.

Jill was very worried, "Jack, what shall we do? The grumps are coming."

"Our only hope is door number fourteen."

"But we can't open it yet, not until tomorrow," said Carol.

"At midnight the steering wheel will light up," Jack reminded them, "We can open it then."

The grumps continued to close in on the sleigh. There were more pairs of glowing eyes and even louder shuffling. Edward's curly white chin hair tingled fiercely and lit up like a beacon. "They're just sad... and lonely. They mean no harm. We can be their friends," he said.

Jill was alarmed, "It's ridiculous. We're so outnumbered. There must be a hundred or more at least. Come on wheel glow... quickly now. We need to open door fourteen."

"They're going to grab us and take us to the sprout fields, anything but the sprout fields," warned Alf.

DOOR FOURTEEN

The grumps' grubby hands were edging ever closer to grabbing the children, but Christmas wouldn't be Christmas without a miracle or two. When it was most needed the steering wheel glowed red. It shone bright and true. The moment Jack saw it, he cried, "The light! Jill open door fourteen, *quickly*!"

She tugged that door so fast and hard that Archie almost toppled over. Inside was an igloo. She grabbed it. In a sparkle and a flash the house of snow covered the whole sleigh and shut out the grumps, but there was more to be done. The igloo had a little arched entrance with a door. It was still open, and a grump or two had crouched down hoping to crawl through it. Their glowing orange eyes looked right inside.

"Oh no you don't," cried Alf. He leapt from the sleigh, quickly slammed the door shut and locked it.

The grumps beyond the door grumbled and moaned but there was nothing they could do for now.

"We did it!" said Alf, punching the air in celebration.

"Jolly good show," said Jack.

"Wasn't it just, we're saved!" cried Jill.

"I knew we would do it!" said Carol.

Archie's latest gift was an extraordinary igloo. It was so much bigger on the inside than out. It had a dome-shaped lounge with an ice chandelier and beanbags, several bedrooms, a sparkling bathroom and kitchen. The beds were incredibly comfortable, with a tiny four-poster for Swish. In a quiet corner sat a low round table and little three-legged stools. It was already laid with cups and saucers and a charming little teapot. There was a card on the table that read, Reserved for the Teddy Bears Picnic. The igloo had windows with red and white striped curtains and little perches for the robins. Next to the entrance was a parking space for the sleigh. Above it was a button marked, Shrink Me with tiny red writing below it that read, 'Only press in an emergency or at dawn'.

Tired children and toys soon settled in their beds, except for Edward. He sat by a window and watched the grumps circling the igloo.

Shuffling along, the grumps repeatedly chanted, "We've come to make you king. It's why we've formed a ring, around your igloo Edward, surrender now give in!"

The others were sleeping soundly, so only Edward heard the grumps calling to him. “They want to make me king,” he mumbled. “Imagine it, me a king?” His chin hair tingled. He was very tempted to leave the igloo and join them. He slowly and quietly moved toward the door, but accidentally knocked over the elf-abet blocks. They tumbled and spelt out the word, ‘F, A, M, I, L, Y’. Edward’s robin flew to his shoulder, nibbled his ear and tweeted.

"My family! What am I doing?" Edward asked himself.

He backed away from the door and sat at the picnic table. He watched Teddy sleeping nearby with Alf. "I love you Teddy. I'm not going anywhere," he said, fiddling with that pesky hair on his chin.

Edward stayed put until sunrise. He did his forty winks trick, snored loudly and immediately woke everyone in the igloo. Soon enough they were all aboard the sleigh and ready to dash on.

"Ready, Teddy, go!" the children cried as Teddy pressed the igloo's Shrink Me button. He found it a little awkward, but there was no stickiness.

Whoosh! The igloo shrank back down to its original size, leaving the sleigh out in the open. It was surrounded by a slushy circle of grump footprints in the snow. "Phew, that was a close one!" whispered Edward. "Dash on, dash on Rocky, but Quietly Does It!" he said, which happened to be the name of their next destination.

As Rocky dashed on they passed less of the fir trees and more of the strange grey rocks. Some rocks had words written on them in slimy green goo. 'Surrender Grump King' they read.

Jill saw them first. "Looks like someone wants the Grump King to surrender," she said.

"Or us. Maybe their king wants *us* to surrender," suggested Nigel.

But Jack knew better, "On the contrary, they are seeking an heir."

"What? Like the one on Edward's chin?" joked Alf.

"No. Jack means they are after an heir to the throne," said Carol, "The grumps want a new king."

"A new king!" mumbled Edward.

"Yes Edward, a new king," confirmed Jack. "But hush now, for we're almost at Quietly Does It."

They soon discovered why it had that name. The way ahead was narrow and lined with steep stone cliffs with many nooks and crannies where the sun never ever shone. Hiding in the shadows were many pairs of glowing orange eyes belonging to grumps waiting for the opportunity to launch an ambush.

Many an elf enjoys a little mischief making and Alf was no different. Sat at the back of the sleigh, he couldn't resist aiming the snowball machine at some of those orange eyes. He set the dial to Super-Sized Snowballs and fired. "It's a snowball gun, not a machine," he whispered. Splat! The first snowball hit its target. Whoosh! Another struck home. That naughty elf was giving the grumps the hump.

He chuckled as his targets were knocked from their hiding places. He must have splattered many a grump before Jack realised what he was up to, but by then it was too late.

As the Santa Bravo Elite sped downhill the grumps hit by snowballs began rolling behind them, gathering speed and turning into giant snowballs as they tumbled.

Jack was furious, "Alf what have you done? Grumps are never happier than when they have the hump. They'll take some stopping now! They'll be meaner and greener than ever."

"But it was fun and they got what they deserved. They shouldn't lock my friends away and put them to work on the sprout farms. Trust me it's no life for an elf."

Swish agreed, "Grumps bad. Bad grumps."

Nigel was alarmed, "Just look at the size of those snowballs... and they're catching up with us!"

"What's happening back there?" asked Edward.

"It's the grumps," cried Carol, "Alf shot some with the snowball machine and now they're tumbling after us, picking up more speed and snow."

Nigel quivered, "They're ginormous and they're going to crash into us any minute."

"Dash on Rocky, dash on!" urged Edward. Rocky pulled with all his might to keep the tumbling grumps from catching them. He led the sleigh out of the narrow path, but the way ahead ended with a sudden steep drop. Caught by surprise, Edward tried hard to stop the sleigh in time. "Whoa Rocky, whoa," he cried, but Rocky skidded causing the sleigh to zigzag from side to side. Unable to slow down, the giant snowballs raced past and rolled over the edge.

"Hang on everyone, we're going over," yelled Edward.

"I can't watch," said Jack, pulling down his lid.

Everyone screamed as they followed the giant snowballs over the edge.

Amazingly, and unknown to the children, the Santa Bravo Elite was designed to glide in an emergency. It did just that, soaring high above Santarctica. The riders could see far into the distance.

On the horizon was a bright white light and sparkling splashes of red, gold and green.

"There ahead, do you see? That's Tinsel Town," said Alf pointing.

"Tinsel Town?" yelled Jill.

"Oh... and this is amazing... we're flying," cried Carol, with the wind in her hair.

Jack dared to look out from under his lid, "Oh my, how exciting. Look at the view. I never knew flying was such fun."

Down to their left and much, much, closer were haunting grey mountains with jagged peaks partly hidden by rising plumes of steam.

"And that, I'm afraid is Bah Humbug," said Alf.

Beneath them was a smooth blanket of snow with just the occasional fir tree. A pair of polar bears looked up at the sleigh as it soared overhead. Further on a group of penguins were huddled about some holes in the snow. Bizarrely, one of the penguins seemed to be fishing with a rod! Alf spotted them. He was much amused and forgot to keep hold of his hat. It caught in the wind, flew off and spiralled behind him. “My hat, not my hat... no!” he cried. They all watched it fall to the ground.

"Don't worry Alf. We can get your hat back when I go on my picnic," said Teddy.

"Good idea Teddy, thank you," Alf replied, as the sleigh dropped closer to the ground.

"We're coming into land, fasten your seat belts," urged Gordon.

"There are no seat belts!" said Alf. "The Santa Bravo Elite doesn't need them."

As he spoke the sleigh came down with a gentle bump and slid gracefully to a halt, right beside a sign that read, 'Quietly Does It'. They were just in time. The daylight was fading and it would be the perfect place to spend the night.

Everyone applauded Edward.

"How utterly thrilling! Can we do it again?" asked Jack with a grinning happy face.

"Round and round in circles, like a teddy bear?" sang Teddy, "One step, two steps, we landed over there."

"Edward, I have to say it, sometimes I'm proud to call you my brother," said Jill.

"I just did it without thinking," he replied.

"Well that's called instinct Edward," said Carol. She came to the front of the sleigh and gave Edward a peck on his cheek.

Edward blushed. He looked back at the towering cliff edge amazed and relieved that they had survived. The grumps they'd left behind weren't at all happy. Those caught up in the giant snowballs were shaken but unharmed. They'd be dizzy for days and right off their sprouts. They vowed their revenge.

***

That evening the igloo became a celebration of the Santa Bravo Elite's maiden flight. The children took turns winding the crank on the gramophone. 'Sleigh Ride' was a clear favourite. They played it several times and Carol and her singers sang a chorus or two, "Come on, it's lovely weather for a sleigh ride together with you. Ding-a-ling a-ling, ding o ling-ding."

Jack was still in a jolly mood, "Though sterner challenges lay ahead, so far this adventure has surprised me. I may have misjudged a few of you. We may get to save Christmas after all." Edward mumbled, "You mean me, don't you Jack? I told you I'm not a grump, didn't I? And I want to win. Maybe you believe me now."

Jack tapped his box and said, "I hope so Edward, for all of us."

DOOR FIFTEEN

Day fifteen started strangely because the grumps had already opened door fifteen and stolen the Christmas pudding. Sitting in the igloo's lounge, Edward flicked door fifteen back and forth with his fingers. "Now you see me, now you don't," he said glumly, as he watched the picture of the pudding.

Jill tried to lighten the mood by wearing her Christmas pudding jumper, but it failed miserably.

"I wonder why they stole the pudding? Jack said grumps only eat sprouts, didn't he?" said Jill.

"And that pudding looks so yummy too," said Gordon.

"Maybe the grumps have a plan," suggested Carol. "They're crafty as well as creepy. I've a feeling they knew what they were doing and took the things they did for a reason. Santa can't deliver any presents without his sack, can he?"

"That's true... and the elves can't make gifts without the letters to Santa, can they Alf? ALF?" Jill called.

But Alf didn't reply, and for good reason. What was that elf up to? Jill searched the igloo. Alf was nowhere to be seen and neither was Teddy, Swish or Jack. She shrieked when she found a note on Teddy's picnic table. It read, 'Gone for a picnic. No children allowed'.

"Edward... Teddy's gone for his picnic," she cried, "With Alf... and the others."

"*Are you kidding me*?" replied Edward, dashing over to Jill. "Let me see that!" he said, grabbing the note. "Teddy having his picnic without me? How could he?"

Edward stomped over to the igloo's Shrink Me button and thumped it. Thwack! Santa's sleigh was back in the open.

"This is Alf's doing," he sneered. "Look there... paw prints in the snow. They can't have gone far. I'll fetch them. I'm going to have serious words with that elf."

"Should I come with you?" asked Carol.

"Best not. It's too risky. Put the igloo back up if you see any grumps."

"Hurry now Edward.... and follow the paw prints right back again. We don't want to lose you," said Jill.

"And be real careful. I saw polar bears out there," warned Nigel.

They watched Edward follow the paw prints up and over a hill until he was no longer in view.

Fretful, Jill accidently knocked over the elf-abet blocks. They rolled and spelt the word, 'B, -, W, A, R, -,' which only made her worry all the more.

***

So, today was the day when Teddy Bear finally had his much longed for picnic. Teddy and Alf had brought Jack and a small picnic basket. Inside the basket was a little teapot, tiny cups and saucers and a patchwork blanket. Swish had hitched a ride on Teddy's shoulder, but Teddy tired quickly, "Must we go much further. I've only little legs and they're tired already. I'm not supposed to get tired until six o'clock. That's when Mummy and Daddy will come to carry me off to bed."

"But we have to go down to the woods for the teddy bear's picnic remember?" said Alf.

"But there are no woods here. It's just snow and mountains and more snow. I'm going to get my blanket out. I'm not taking one more step. I'm supposed to be having a lovely time today."

"But Teddy, I need to get my hat back."

Teddy was defiant. He took his blanket out and laid it on the snow. He sat down and began to organise his tea set. Alf gave in and put Jack on the blanket.

Jack came out of his box, looking very serious, "Teddy has waited so long for this picnic. Don't spoil it for him. Just do what he says, please Alf."

"Okay, but afterwards I'm going to look for my hat."

"Teddy bear's picnic, picnic bear's Teddy," said Swish softly as she pirouetted on the blanket.

"Tea anyone? I'll pour," asked Teddy happily. He took some pretend sips from a cup.

"But where's my treacle? Alf, you promised me treacle," said Jack.

"Look, Teddy wanted you to come. I had to say something... anyway you don't eat anything do you?"

"That's not the point," replied Jack, "It's the principle of the thing."

Teddy stood up, "I'm going to gaily gad about, play and SHOUT."

The sudden loud noise startled Swish and she flew away.

"Shush Teddy," urged Jack, "You frightened Swish and the grumps will hear you."

Teddy shook his head, "This wouldn't have happened if Edward had come. Why didn't he come? Alf, you said he would. Where is he?"

Alf smiled his cheeky grin. What was he up to?

***

Teddy's cry of SHOUT echoed about Santarctica. Edward heard it. He knew the toys couldn't be far away. He trudged through the soft snow and spotted them at the top of a hill. Teddy waved at Edward and so did someone else. It was a tall figure that appeared in the shadow of a rock wearing what looked like a brown shaggy coat, clumpy boots, a squidgy green face mask and sunglasses.

"Aphrodite, is that really you?" called Edward.

He tramped awkwardly towards her.

"How wonderful Edward. We've... I've come to get you," said the figure. The voice was gruff and unlike Aphrodite's.

"*Get me*? What does that mean? And have you been eating sprouts again? I can smell them."

"Sprouts, yum... It's easy-peasy. We need you." But then a voice spoke from the figure's tummy, "No numbskull, it's 'I need you', not 'we need you'." The figure cleared its throat, "A-hum, oh yes. *I need you*."

"Hang on. You're not Aphrodite," said Edward, but by then it was already too late. The grumps threw off their disguise. Several of them were sat on each other's shoulders. One held a large sack labelled Santa.

The grumps pounced on Edward, covered him with the sack and tied the top. Edward struggled hard, but because Alf had snowballed them the grumps had the serious hump. It made them meaner and greener. There was no escape for Edward.

"Surrender grump king," they cried.

"*Never*. Let me go!"

Swish was nearby, "Grumps. Let go Edward. Edward let go," she urged. But they hardly heard her and she was too fragile and small to help.

***

Teddy witnessed everything, "Oh my, there's the 'big surprise' and the 'going in disguise'. Poor Edward. This has not been a lovely picnic, not one bit of it."

Jack turned to Alf and said, "You Alf gave the grumps the hump on purpose, didn't you? Now look, they're dragging Edward off in Santa's sack to Bah Humbug."

Alf didn't reply. Instead, he pushed down Jack's lid. Picked him up and began to head back to the sleigh. Jack struggled and pushed hard at his lid, but Alf kept it held firmly shut.

Jack cried with a muffled voice, "What are you going to do with me? Where are you taking me?"

"Quiet Zebedee, I know what I'm doing. If you say one word about this to the others I'll break that spring of yours for good. Do you understand?"

Teddy was dumbstruck by what had happened to Edward, so didn't listen to what Alf said to Jack. In all innocence, he asked, "Are you going to look for your hat now? Are you taking Jack too?"

"I don't care about my hat," he replied.

"Well I care about my Edward even if he was late for my picnic. I'm going to rescue him." He stood up and took slow weary steps in the direction the grumps had taken.

"Good luck with that. You'll need it. Either you'll freeze or the grumps will get you and tear your stuffing out. I'd give up and return to the sleigh with us if I were you," said Alf as he began to head back.

But Teddy kept going. He was one hundred and ten percent focused on rescuing Edward that he failed to notice some nearby penguins. One of the penguins was holding a green elf hat and showing it to his friends.

"There, what did I tell you? I told you I saw something fall from the sky, but you wouldn't believe me, *oh no*. That's a fishy tale you said."

"It's an elves hat!" replied a second penguin.

"Well how did it get here, you tell me that, eh? Elves can't fly. Maybe that's it. If I put this hat on I'll be able to fly too. Here let me have it," asked the first penguin.

"Hang on Prancer. There's a name tag inside it. This is Alf's hat."

"He gave me his fishing rod, did Alf," said a third penguin.

"Please Blitzen, give it to me. I have to try."

Prancer the penguin took the hat, placed it on his head and waddled about flapping his flippers.

"I just need to go a bit faster, that'll do it," Prancer said, as he skidded about in a circle only to slip onto his bottom.

"Stop fooling around," said the third penguin, "Alf was kind to us. He's a good elf, one of the best! I say we find him and give it back. Let's take it to his tree house."

Prancer got to his feet and brushed himself down, "Yeah. That stupid rod doesn't work. We dangled it for days and not one fish has climbed on to that hook. It's broken, that's what it is... either that or the fish know."

A fourth penguin spoke, "I'm sure those fish are getting smarter."

"I'm talking about the hat, not the fishing rod," said the third penguin.

"Okay, let's take it back, but let me have one more go," said Prancer. "I know I can fly. I can feel it in my feathers. I'll fly right up to the tree house."

***

A frightened Swish had flown quickly back to the sleigh. The children immediately knew something was terribly wrong.

"What's happened Swish? Where's Edward and the others?" asked Jill.

"Grumps come. Grumps bad. Bad grumps," swished Swish.

"Swish, what did the grumps do?" asked Carol.

"Grab Edward grumps."

"No, not my brother, not Edward? The blocks said 'beware', I should have called him back."

Gordon shook his head, "I should have gone with him. It's all my fault... *again*."

"I just knew something terrible would happen," said Nigel, losing all his optimism.

"Shut up you two!" snapped Jill fiercely. "How exactly is that *helping*?"

Shortly after the 'telling-off', Alf appeared carrying Jack and pretending to be shaken up.

"It was the grumps," said Alf, "They took Edward... and Teddy. They were disguised as Aphrodite. He didn't have a chance. They ambushed him and dragged him off in Santa's sack. I think they're taking him... I mean, them... to Bah Humbug. We were helpless to stop them."

"*Teddy go*? Swish sad... Sad Swish."

"Now this really is without any doubt whatsoever the worst day I've ever known. I've seriously had enough of this dream. I want to wake up," said Jill. She pinched herself, but the dream continued.

Jack crawled out of his box. He had a tearful face. "Jill, hug me," he said. Jill immediately took her favourite old toy off Alf and started to cry.

"Please don't cry," said Jack, "Remember... grumps can't hurt children. It's in Santa Clause eight. *If* they play by the rules Edward shouldn't come to any harm."

"*If*?" replied Jill.

"I'm sorry. There was nothing we could do to stop them, was there Jack?" added Alf, but Jack didn't reply.

"Well. It's too late to do anything about it now," said Carol. "I suggest we stay here tonight and travel to Bah Humbug first thing in the morning. I've a feeling that whatever comes out of Archie's door tomorrow will help save them from the grumps."

Jill agreed, "I think you're right Carol. It's much too dangerous."

So they set up the igloo once more.

***

As the sun began to drop lower in the sky, poor Teddy was slowly making his lonely and weary way towards Bah Humbug. He was one brave tatty Teddy. There was a look on his face that Edward had also shown - determination. Alas, determination alone might not be enough for as darkness fell the grumps saw Teddy and closed in on him. Teddy was a simple soft target. He was just an innocent bear stuffed with fluff.

"Hey there lonely bear, what you doing?" asked a grump.

"I'm going to Bah Humbug."

"Isn't it past your bedtime?" asked another grump.

"I don't care. I'm going to rescue Edward."

"But six o'clock has come and gone bear," said a third grump.

Teddy stopped in his tracks, "Has it? Mummy and Daddy were supposed to come and get me."

"Poor Baby Bear," joked the first grump.

"All simple and stuffed with fluff," teased the second.

"With an ear hanging off," added a third.

"Leave my ear out of this. I'm not afraid of you or any grump. I'm not afraid of anything."

"Any last words bear, before we rip your stuffing out?" said the first grump menacingly.

Luckily, just as all seemed lost for Teddy, Christmas miracle number two happened.

"Leave the bear alone!" said a booming voice. It belonged to a huge polar bear.

The grumps turned around to find two polar bears towering over them ready to strike.

The frightened grumps backed away nervously.

"It was only a game," said the first.

"We don't even like stuffing. We only eat sprouts."

"We like teddy bears, honest," said the third.

They were feeble excuses, so the polar bears roared. The grumps fled as quickly as they could, which wasn't very fast at all.

Teddy leaned back and looked up at his rescuers, "Are you Mummy and Daddy Bear? I had my picnic. I'm very tired now and it's past six o'clock."

Daddy Bear replied, "Don't worry little one. We'll look after you." He got down on all fours, "Climb up on my back. We know somewhere cosy with a nice warm bed."

"And I'll make us some lovely porridge first thing in the morning. Not too hot, not too cold, but just right," promised Mummy Bear.

DOOR SIXTEEN

Teddy awoke in the arms of Mummy and Daddy Bear then enjoyed the most perfect bowl of porridge. His paws got terribly sticky once more, but he didn't care one bit.

Back at the igloo things were much more stressful. The children had struggled to sleep because they were so worried about Edward and Teddy. Jack was strangely quiet and Swish was now very suspicious of Alf, but it was a new day and a new door. Jill opened door sixteen and reached inside. She pulled out a bright green sprig of mistletoe with waxy white berries.

"It's mistletoe. What use is this?" said Jill disappointedly.

Jack explained, "Tradition has it that you're supposed to kiss someone you like under it, so pucker up."

"Not now Jack," Jill replied.

"Maybe I was wrong about door sixteen," mumbled Carol.

"What are we going to do?" asked Nigel.

Alf had a plan, "We carry on, that's what. Let's go to Bah Humbug and rescue Edward and get all the stuff back... and the sooner the better."

"Shush elf. You got us into this mess in the first place. Edward's my brother. It's my job to look after him. I'll decide what happens next," said Jill.

But Alf was in the mood to argue, "He's not a baby and who put you in charge? You're not the one wearing the crown, she is." He pointed his bony finger at Carol.

"It's not a real crown Alf. It's only made of paper. Where's the elf-abet blocks. Let's see what they have to say?" said Jill. She found the blocks and rolled them. They read, 'R, -, S, C, U, -'.

"That settles it... and I'm going to drive. It's what Edward would have wanted." She pressed the 'Shrink Me' button and typed 'Bah Humbug' into the Santa. Nav.

***

At Bah Humbug there was tremendous excitement. Edward was held prisoner at the heart of the grumps' world. Stripped of his Christmas teddy jumper, Edward had been tied to a big slimy stone throne slap-bang in the middle of a huge domed chamber. Before him was an old wooden chest with a chunky brass lock. Unable to wriggle free, he looked around the chamber. There was a crumbling balcony running around the inside of the dome. Hanging from it were twenty-five numbered orange lanterns, with lantern number sixteen glowing the brightest.

There were many grumps standing on the balcony staring right at Edward and many more of the stumpy green creatures gathering in the chamber. Others shuffled in from the many corridors that fed it, adding to the throng. A stench of boiling sprouts wafted in with them. The grumps all looked much the same, except for a few who wore golden medallions around their necks. The grump with the largest medallion, which had the letters AAA engraved ornately on it, stepped forward and addressed the hoard.

"Fellow grumps, look who we have here."

"EDWARD!" shouted the grumps, all together.

"I promised you, didn't I? And General Grump keeps his promises, doesn't he? What do you say to that?"

"We're happy being grumps!" they chanted.

The General grabbed a goblet from the top of the wooden chest. The goblet held a sludgy stinky green liquid. He offered it to Edward, "We're happy being grumps. Celebrate with us. Drink Edward, drink."

"Ten times *yuk*! What is it?"

"Vintage Sprout Supreme... It's thirty years old."

Edward scrunched up his face, "It looks disgusting. It smells disgusting. Get it away from me."

But the General kept holding the goblet right under Edward's nose, trying to tempt him to take a sip.

"Why am I here? What do you want from me?" asked Edward, pulling against the ropes.

"You already know. You feel it in your bones. Why you even have a picture of an angry grump on your shirt."

Angrily, Edward replied, "Hey... that's not a grump, that's a superhero!"

"But you could be one too, if you became our King!"

The watching grumps chanted, "Grump King! Grump King! Grump King!"

Edward cried, "I'm not one of you. I don't much like Christmas, I admit. But I have a really good reason for that. It doesn't make me a grump and definitely *not* your king. Let me go. I want to be with my friends."

"Oh, don't worry, that's being arranged," said the General with an evil grin.

"You leave my friends out of this!"

General Grump stood right in front of Edward. He stared deep into his eyes, "It's not my doing. They're like moths to a flame. Forget them. We have so much to offer you." He turned to face his fellow grumps and raised his hands, "Feel the beat of the Grump Grumble. Listen. It calls to you."

The grumps formed a circle and marched about the throne. They chanted the Grump Grumble,

The Grump Grumble

"I'm happy being a grump.
I'm happy having the hump.
We don't like Christmas, not one bit.
Santa and his sleigh can up and fly away.
We don't like Christmas, not one bit.
His elves have got the sack, and they won't be coming back.
We don't like Christmas, not one bit.

Not at all, not at all.
Not at all, not at all.
Not one single little piece of it at all, not one bit!

I'm happy being a grump.
I'm happy having the hump.
We don't like Christmas, not one bit.
Rudolph's broke his nose and it no longer glows.
We don't like Christmas not one bit.
No presents for any of you, no matter what you do.
We don't like Christmas, not one bit. Not one little bit."

Edward whispered, "Not one bit."

The chanting echoed throughout a labyrinth of dark tunnels and into cold damp cells where many elves were held prisoner. It spread to row upon row of sprout bushes tended to by more captured elves, and finally to the rusty gated entrance to Bah Humbug. Above the gate was the grump motto, 'Misery is Joy'.

On each side of the gate were big spiky orange lanterns. A shredded Christmas teddy jumper hung from one of them. It had belonged to Edward. The many grumps guarding the elves, the sprout fields and fortress gates joined in with the Grump Grumble.

General Grump grinned and offered Edward the goblet again, "You feel it don't you. Now drink from the General's goblet."

Edward took a mouthful of Sprout Supreme. Would he ever be the same again?

The grumps chanting reached the Santa Bravo Elite. The sleigh had only just arrived at the perfect place from which to secretly spy on Bah Humbug. Alf knew the land well and had guided them to a spot up on high and overlooking the fortress. His tree house was just above them and there were lots of holly bushes in which to hide the sleigh. They could see the rusty old gates, the sprout fields, a playground with broken swings and slides, and towering crooked grey stone chimneys which spewed steam night and day. No snow fell there and nothing would grow except sprouts.

A ring of jingle bells surrounded the whole of Bah Humbug to keep the grimness in and the joyfulness out. It was a miserable and soulless place where hope and happiness had been banished.

Whenever the grumps chanted the fortress grew a little bigger and a little more miserable. Things were looking bleak for Edward and all the children in the world that loved Christmas. But this dream belonged to the children of Conjuring Cottage and they would never surrender.

"Did you hear that? It's the grumps," said Jill.

"It sounds like they're celebrating. Edward must be inside," replied Carol.

"Well I know Edward, he won't give in easily and neither should we. Let's get him out of there," said Jill.

Nigel was less confident, "Just look at that place. There are guards and everything. How ever are we going to do it?"

Jack agreed, "We need a fool proof plan, that's how. They'll be expecting us and it depends on whether we can trust Alf. Can we trust you Alf?"

Alf shrugged his shoulders, "You've no choice. I'm your best hope. The grumps kept me prisoner in their fortress for weeks. I was one of the lucky ones. I escaped. I know the inside of Bah Humbug like the back of my hand, every secret corridor, trap door and prison cell."

"And if you got out then you can get back in again," suggested Jill.

"Spot on! When I escaped I promised to return and set my brother elves free, every last one of them."

Jack wasn't convinced, "So you say, I wonder if Teddy's in there too. Do you wonder that Alf, *do you*?"

Swish swished, "Teddy love. Love Teddy."

"Do you know, I've a feeling Teddy will turn up again when we least expect it," said Carol.

***

Teddy had been lost in the moment. Mummy Bear and Daddy Bear had spoilt him rotten with a glorious picnic in one of the loveliest parts of Santarctica. Then he remembered about Edward, “Oh my, I almost forgot. I must go rescue Edward.”

“Who's Edward?” asked Mummy Bear.

“Edward? Why Santa Claus gave me to him for Christmas. He's a lost boy and the grumps took him. He's in Bah Humbug. I was going to rescue him when you rescued me.”

“Edward you say?” asked Daddy Bear, “He’s the one everyone is talking about. Why didn't you tell us this before? This means we don't have much time. Hop up on my back Baby Bear. We have work to do.”

***

That evening, inside the igloo, the children thought about all of Archie’s gifts and the odd things Aphrodite had put on the sleigh. Jack had told them that they would need to use everything wisely including, the scented candles in Soggy Sprout Farts, Smiley Happy Faces and Gooey Ear Wax, the everlasting gloopy green face mask, Clementine oranges, mistletoe, a map of Santarctica, the gramophone, a snowball-making machine, a jack-in-the-box with a poor memory and broken spring, a mischievous elf, robins, a fairy, elf-abet blocks and a rocking horse. Teddy was missing, so was his tea set and the Santa Sweet.

All they had to do was break into Bah Humbug unnoticed, avoid capture, find and recover the stolen gifts, rescue Edward and reach Tinsel Town by Christmas Day. Winning at Archie’s Advent Adventure couldn’t be simpler... could it?

DOOR SEVENTEEN

In Edward's absence, Jill had no choice but to open door seventeen. She had her fingers crossed for something spectacular. Inside was a little drummer boy dressed in a traditional soldiers outfit. He wore a sparkling red jacket, white trousers and long black boots. On his head was a tall furry Busby hat. The drum hung on a sash around his neck and he held two drum sticks. Jill placed him on the igloo floor. In a sparkle and a flash the drummer boy grew bigger. Taller, in fact, than the other children and by quite some bit. He wiggled his fake moustache, ripped it off in disgust and threw it to the floor.

"Hey man. What's going down?" he said, sounding really cool.

"Where shall we start?" asked Jill.

"With a groove baby. Hey this is far out. Shall I play for you? *Pa rum pa pa rum*, on my drum?" he said, bashing his drum. The sound sent Swish flying about the igloo.

"I know that tune. It's the Little Drummer Boy, but you're not very..." said Carol.

"Little? I know. It's a bash," replied the boy before continuing to play.

Carol sang along, "Come they told me, pa rum pa pa rum. A new born king to see pa rum pa pa rum." Nigel and Gordon sang along, "Our finest gifts we bring, pa rum pa pa rum. To lay before the king, pa rum pa pa rum."

Jack was watching on in disbelief. He had a frowning face with an open mouth, "That's perfect, really helpful, a child with a drum in a sparkly red jacket. What better way to let the grumps know we're here. Where's my white flag of surrender? I want to wave it now. Please somebody put me out of my misery."

"Don't mind him. His spring's just a bit wonky!" said Jill.

"Hey, the dude's out of tune and he lives in a box. That's totally square."

"Far out man!" replied Jack. He was being ironic.
"What's your name?" asked Carol.
"I'm Dylan baby. Do you dig it?"
"I think I'll call you Dummer Boy," said Jack.

***

Not far away in Bah Humbug, Edward was no longer tied to the throne. General Grump was giving him a tour of the many tunnels and rooms in the fortress, but kept him well away from the cells where countless elves were held prisoner. Edward had no idea if it was day or night for the fortress was in constant gloom. He wasn't at all afraid of the strange lava like blocks that heated the cauldrons of boiling sprouts. They helped him make his way as did the light from his glowing white chin hair.

Wherever he went in the fortress, grumps would bow and say, 'Hail the new Grump King'. In a small chamber a group of grumps were sitting, debating and grumbling,
"Christmas? So much for ho, ho, ho. How about no, no, no?" said one.
"It's such a terrible waste of money and effort for just one day," said a second.
"And the children never appreciate any of it. I want... I want... I want!" grumbled a third.
"And the letters to Santa... such terrible grammar and spelling," added the first grump.
"And the dumb decorations. Tinsel, I really hate it," mumbled the second.
"I can't wait until it's all over, when Christmas is cancelled forever. Imagine it, no more Christmas pudding bringing joy to the world."
"As for that fat old man in the ridiculous red suit, he looks like a wrinkly old tomato," said the third grump.

A few of the grumps sniggered, if only for a second or two for laughter and merriment had no place at Bah Humbug.

"Santa, he's just a fake and a fraud. You don't believe in Father Christmas either, do you Edward?" said General Grump, looking straight at Edward, but Edward stayed silent.

"You don't say much do you Edward. What's up? Kat got your tongue?"

"Ah Kat... and Aphrodite!" said Edward quietly.

"Forget her Edward. She's crazy... wackadoodle," said General Grump.

"Weird, yes? Wackadoodle, no? She's kind and special... and as for you grumps, I understand you. Christmas can be a miserable time for the lonely and the broken hearted."

"The lonely... yes the lonely," said a grump, with his head bowed.

"And the broken hearted," added another, "And the unwanted."

General Grump snapped, "Enough. *Misery is joy*. Do you know, the thing I hate most about Christmas is the carol singers. 'O' Come all ye faithful'... utter drivel."

Edward interrupted, "Joyful and triumphant... *Carol*! I need to get out of here. I want to be with my friends."

"We're your friends now Edward... GUARDS!"

***

Dylan's arrival didn't appear to help much with plans for a rescue mission. All he did was bang on about his dream of being in a famous band, "And then I'm going to throw a gig right. It'll be so cool. There'll be dancing chicks and swingers. It'll be totally awesome."

"I always wanted to play guitar," said Alf, practicing 'air guitar' by pretending to play an imaginary one.

Jack wisecracked, "Do you by chance know, 'Pop Goes the Weasel'? It's such a classic."

"That's all very well for you Dylan but we're really trying to come up with a plan to get my brother out of Bah Humbug," said Jill.

"Where's that at?" asked Dylan.

"Outside, that's where," said Carol. "If you press the Shrink Me button, you'll see."

So Dylan did just that. Once the igloo had shrunk, Nigel warned him, "You need to keep real quiet... no drumming. The grumps don't know we're here."

Dylan looked at the gloomy grey fortress and watched the smoke rise from the many crooked chimneys. He noticed the sign, 'Misery is Joy' above the gates.

"Oooh, they're smoking! Those guys... what're they on?" he asked.

"It's the grumps doing. They're the creepy little critters that took Edward," said Gordon.

Swish swished, "Grumps bad. Bad grumps."

Dylan asked, "Do the grumps like bears? Polar bears?"

"No... of course not Dummer Boy," said Jack.

"Well then why are The Three Bears at the gate?"

"What did you say?" asked Jill.

Dylan was spot on. Mummy and Daddy Bear were at the Bah Humbug gates with Teddy.

"That's Teddy, I'm sure of it," said Jill. "But it doesn't make sense. Alf, you said the grumps had Teddy. You said they took him." She turned to gawp at Alf, "*Didn't you*?"

"Yes he did say that, *didn't he*?" said Jack knowingly.

Alf gave a sheepish smile.

***

Teddy and his new friends were indeed walking up to the gates of Bah Humbug. The startled guards didn't know quite what to do.

"It's The Three Bears... no sign of Goldilocks though."

"I can see that Jasper. What does the guard rule book say about bears?"

"I don't think it says anything about bears Bandit."

The bears reached the gate.

Teddy climbed down from Daddy Bear's back.

"What do you want bear? Goldilocks doesn't live here," said Bandit.

"Good one Bandit. That's just what I was gonna say."

Teddy spoke, "We're not looking for Goldilocks. We've come to rescue Edward. I'm his teddy."

Bandit laughed and said, "Your Edward's teddy and you've come to rescue him?"

Jasper nudged his fellow guard, "Our new king has a teddy? Can you believe it?"

Bandit was still laughing, "He's got to be too old for a tatty old bear!"

Teddy put his paws on his hips and growled, "It's *not* funny and grumps aren't supposed to laugh."

"Who says? Nobody's watching us are they?" said Bandit.

"And anyway, Edward loves me," said Teddy.

Daddy Bear put a stop to the grumps' fun, "You're never too old for a teddy. Now are you going to let us in or not? Look at me." He stood up and looked down on them, "I'm big and you're small."

"You are very big!" agreed Jasper. "I'm thinking. The rule book doesn't say anything about polar bears."

"Jasper, we could just let them in. It's not breaking any rules."

"We could. You're right. That's perfect. Good thinking Bandit."

"No problem. And they won't get far. Its dark inside and there's so many tunnels. They'll get lost anyway. It'll be the last we see of them."

"Okay," said Jasper, "We've decided you can go in, but don't blame us if you never come back out again."

"Yes. Don't say we didn't warn you."

They opened the gates and the bears went through.

"Would you believe it, not even a thank you," said Jasper.

"We'll just have to grin and bear it... get it? Grin and *bear* it?"

Jasper smirked, "Stop it. You're making me laugh. Teddy was right, us grumps aren't supposed to laugh."

***

Way up on the hill, the children saw the bears enter the grounds of the fortress.

"Teddy's just gone into Bah Humbug... That's one brave Teddy," said Jill.

"Chill out! If I had polar bears as friends I'd be brave too," said Dylan casually.

"I've a nasty feeling about this," mumbled Carol.

"What should we do? Should we follow him? Blast, where are those elf-abet blocks?" said Jill. She grabbed then rolled them. They spelt, 'R, -, V, -, A, L'.

Dylan gave the blocks the thumbs down, "Heavy, the bricks got no Es."

"'Reveal'? What does that mean?" asked Jill.

Jack began, "Reveal means tell, or disclose. Make previously unknown or secret information available to others. It is..."

Jill interrupted him, "I know that, it just doesn't make sense!"

Right on cue the penguins arrived with Alf's hat and fishing rod. They also had Teddy's picnic basket and Prancer was wearing sunglasses.

"Ah, Alf we found you," said Blitzen, "Right under your tree house as we'd hoped."

"You'll never guess. I've been trying to fly in your hat. Can I have one more go? I want to try to fly up to your tree house," said Prancer.

"There's a tree house?" asked Nigel, "Where?"

"Up there," said Prancer as he leaned back. He lost his balance and fell on to his bottom. The sunglasses fell off.

Dylan performed a soft drum roll, "You guys are wicked. I love the shades Man."

Blitzen was confused, "Us wicked? Absolutely not! We're just like Alf. He's the Master Elf you know, did he tell you?"

"No Blitzen, I didn't... It's no big deal," said Alf.

"Oh, why not?" Prancer asked. "Aren't these your friends?" He got to his feet and offered the sunglasses to Dylan.

"Right on!" he said, happily taking them.

"Alf came out of one of Archie's doors? He's part of our adventure," said Jill, smiling widely because she was in conversation with a penguin.

"He's good at getting in and out of tight places, aren't you Alf," said another penguin.

"It's a delight to meet you little guys, but we're in the middle of something really important," said Jill, but her amusement quickly disappeared when she recognised Teddy's picnic basket, "Where did you get that?"

"We found it near Alf's hat. We wondered if that fell out of the sky too," said a penguin.

"I told them about the hat. They didn't believe me. They do now," added Prancer smugly.

"It's Edward's Teddy's picnic basket," said Jill.

"Who's Edward Teddy?" asked Prancer.

Alf just wanted the penguins to leave, "It's a long story. Well Blitzen, Prancer, you guys, thanks for popping by and returning my hat, but as Jill said we really are very busy right now, so..."

"Blitzen and Prancer? They're Santa's reindeer names," said Carol curiously.

Prancer flapped his flippers and waddled over to Alf and asked, "Alf you haven't told us if General Grump is going to release all the elves now that you helped them catch the new grump king. Is he going to? Is that why you're here? Are you waiting for them?"

"*Blabbermouth*!" snarled Alf.

"Is this TRUE Alf?" snapped Jill. "You knew the grumps were waiting for Edward, didn't you? You took the toys on a picnic knowing he would go looking for them. I bet you unbolted the door at Conjuring Cottage so the grumps could get in and steal the gifts. It's skulduggery. *What have you done Alf?"*

Alf shrugged his shoulders, "Saved my fellow elves, that's what. They've turned too many into grumps. I had to do something."

Jill screwed up her face in dismay, "Turning them into grumps? Are you *serious*?"

Jack wanted his revenge on Alf, "I knew it. You foolish gullible elf, do you really think they'll let them all go?"

"But General Grump promised. It's why they let me go. And yes, I'm serious. It's the Sprout Supreme that does it."

"Sprout Supreme? How dare you Alf, Edward's my brother!" cried Jill. She was furious.

"Well he hates Christmas. He told me so himself. He's just what they're looking for."

Blitzen tried to calm things down, "It's not going well is it? Will the fishing rod help?"

"It doesn't work. We can't get a single fish to swim on to the hook," said another of the penguins.

"Dasher... you're supposed to put bait on it," said Alf.

"Bait?" asked Dasher.

"A worm."

"I knew it," said Prancer, "I told them, but they wouldn't listen. No one listens to me. Why do I bother?"

Jack took another swipe at the elf, "Alf, you've been fished in, hook, line and sinker. You've given the grumps what they want and unless we do something Christmas will be cancelled forever."

"No way man. That's so heavy," said Dylan, modelling the sunglasses.

"Alf, what do you want me to do with your hat?" asked Blitzen.

"I don't care about my stupid hat! Keep it!"

***

Deep within Bah Humbug Teddy and the polar bears were slowly making their way through the tunnels. No grump dared stop them, but tried their best to warn others about the intruders.

"Watch out there are bears about," warned a grump, calling out.

"Just keep away from my sprouts... they're my sprouts," said another.

"Yucky stinky sprouts. Where's Edward?" asked Teddy politely.

"Sorry... can't hear you bear."

Teddy spoke louder, "I said, 'Where's my Edward?'"

The grump scratched his head, "Your Edward? A Teddy for Eddie."

"Eddie's Teddy?" added another.

"A Ted for Ed," said a third.

Teddy growled, "Stop that. It's so dull. Now where is he?"

"Don't growl at me bear."

Daddy Bear spoke, "That's not a growl, this is a growl WHERE'S EDWARD?" His roar shook the walls of the fortress and made the cauldrons rattle. The grumps covered their ears. One said, "We could just tell him. No one will know."

Another grump said, "The new Grump King is with the General."

"My Edward's not the Grump King. He's my Edward," said Teddy.

"Ah, who cares what you think, stupid bear. Say hello to Red Riding Hood for me."

"Who you calling stupid? I'm not the one who picked the wrong fairy tale," replied Teddy, as he walked away.

The bears travelled deeper into Bah Humbug. They passed cells with many elves being force fed revolting stinky green liquid. A grump guard warned, "Polar bears approaching."

Teddy didn't like what he saw, "Leave the elves alone. They're only small."

"And so are you... no bears allowed," said a smirking guard. "Oh, but they're not small," he added as the big bears turned the corner, "Eh... it's just the General's orders. Who are you? What do you want?" asked the guard.

"I'm Edward's Teddy. We've come to rescue him."

"Hey Oscar, it's Eddie's Teddy?"

"Tedward for short," said Oscar the Grump.

"Not again! It's getting so darn boring," said Teddy.

"And annoying. Let the elves go," ordered Mummy Bear.

"No, sorry, we're not allowed to... we're following orders."

"Well *DON'T*!" growled Daddy Bear.

Startled, many of the grumps dropped their goblets, spilling slimy green liquid everywhere.

"That was Sprout Supreme. What a terrible waste, and just look at the mess," said Oscar.

"Just wait for the mess I'll make when we return," replied Daddy Bear.

"Sound the alarm!" cried a nervous grump.

"Eh, we don't have an alarm, you dipstick."

"Don't we? Oh... don't sound the alarm then!"

The bears marched on.

The grumps had taken Edward back to the main chamber and tied him to the throne once more. Several of the stumpy green creatures stood idly about watching and listening to the General.

"Surrender Edward. Drink," said the General presenting him with another goblet of Sprout Supreme.

"You're not listening to me, 'I don't want to be Grump King'. Choose someone else."

"Impossible. Only a real boy who doesn't believe in Father Christmas can become Grump King. And you don't believe in him, do you Edward?" asked General Grump sneering.

"You won't make me say it."

"The game's up Edward. All the odds are stacked against you. You'll never win... we have the stolen gifts and I'm told you've lost the Santa Sweet. Jack already believes you're one of us. Alf is on our side. Your sister bosses you about and... worst of all, your father thinks you're too old for a teddy and you should grow up fast. Oh, and that bear with one ear didn't even want you on his picnic, did he?"

"What are you talking about? Alf isn't on your side?" argued Edward.

"Oh yes he is. He snowballed the grumps *on purpose* to give them the hump and make them meaner. He took your teddy on a picnic *on purpose* because he knew you would follow him. He led you right into our trap. He also unbolted the door *on purpose* to let us into the cottage so we could steal the gifts. And do you know what's so ironic... it's all here in this chest."

He tapped the top of the chest, "So close, yet so far away and my medallion here is the key... A, A, A." He held the medal up to tease Edward with it, "For Archie's Advent Adventure... and you lose!"

Edward was so angry, "I knew that darn elf couldn't be trusted. He called me Buddy. I'm not his buddy. If I ever see that elf again, I'll... I'll."

"Alf betrayed you, but the truth is all elves can't be trusted. They're nothing but bother. What's the point of them? They're all better off as grumps," said General Grump.

"Bother, that's just what the elf-abet blocks said."

"Drink Edward," insisted General Grump, as he put the goblet to Edward's lips again. Reluctantly, Edward drank all of the Sprout Supreme.

He'd just swallowed the last drop when Teddy and the polar bears entered the chamber.

"Teddy, is that *you*?" Edward asked in astonishment.

"Hello Edward. I've come to rescue you."

"*You have*? You brave tatty old bear," spluttered Edward.

General Grump wisecracked, "Oh my, it's The Three Bears. Where's goldilocks?"

"Not again! Leave her out of this... you slimy stinky nincompoop... and let my Edward go," said Teddy.

The nervous grumps in the chamber parted as the bears moved closer to Edward.

"I see you have some new friends," said Edward, trying to loosen the ropes that tied him.

"They're Mummy and Daddy Bear. They picked me up at six o'clock and took me home to bed."

"Thank you... so much," said Edward to the polar bears.

"Edward's Teddy's bears, bears for Eddie's Teddy, Ed's Ted's bears, Tedward's bears for short," sneered General Grump.

Teddy shook his head. "Claptrap! Is there no escape from it?" he asked.

"Clap-trap? Indeed, come closer bears," asked General Grump. "Let me get a good look at these two mighty beasts who dare to enter my fortress."

The polar bears came forward, completely unaware that they both now stood right on top of a big trap door.

"Such powerful creatures... pity!" whispered the General.

He pulled a lever beside the chest. The trap door swung open and the polar bears tumbled into a pit. They roared and leapt up but were unable to get out before the trap doors slammed shut again.

"Clap-trap!" cried General Grump, urging all the grumps to do so. They clapped wildly.

"A glorious defeat! So close but yet so far. It pains me. Poor mighty bears undone by a mere grump," announced the General. He thumped his chest in triumph, hurting his hands, "Ouch," he squealed.

A shocked Teddy cried, "What did you do? Mummy Bear, Daddy Bear... let them go."

"No... no you can't do that to them," uttered Edward.

"I just did! Their days of good deed doing are *over*," replied General Grump smugly.

The watching grumps cheered again then chanted, "I'm happy being a grump. I'm happy having the hump. We don't like Christmas, not one bit."

The chanting spread about the tunnels and beyond.

"Well I happen to like it! Santa gave me to Edward for his first Christmas," said Teddy bravely.

"He did Teddy... and I've loved you every day since."

"Ah," said General Grump. "How sweet. So you love this bear do you? Let's put that to the test shall we Edward. Guards, grab that teddy."

"No, leave him alone."

The guards grabbed Teddy and led him over to General Grump, "Tatty, isn't he? And look at that ear, it's almost fallen off. Shall we give him a matching pair?" The General gently stroked Teddy's torn ear. He took a good look at it.

"Get off me. You stinky, sticky, mucky poops," snapped Teddy angrily. One of the grump guards began to tug at his good ear.

"Ouch, *ouch*, Edward help me!" squealed Teddy.

"LET TEDDY GO" shouted Edward.

"You can make it stop Edward. Just say those words. Tell us you don't believe in Father Christmas. Surrender Grump King. You can keep your Teddy afterwards for as long as you like and we'll fix this torn... ear... I promise."

"Don't say it Edward. *Don't*."

The grumps pulled at his good ear again. The stitching began to undo and stuffing appeared. General Grump still had hold of the bad ear.

"No Teddy, no... Okay, I'll say it. *'I don't believe in Father Christmas!'*"

Everyone froze. What would happen now? Would Edward wake up? Was the adventure over? No, it was worse than that, much worse. Edward changed into a grump. His legs shrunk. His nose grew and his eyes turned orange.

"Edward, no!"

The grumps let Teddy go. He slumped to the floor and cried. General Grump let him be.

"A new born king to see pa rum pa pa rum!" sang General Grump.

The ecstatic grumps chanted, "Grump King! Grump King! Grump King!"

"Now for your coronation. The golden paper crown from the cracker, do you have it Edward? It will seal your fate as Grump King forever."

"No. I gave it to Carol. It's stuck on her big stupid head," he grumbled meanly.

"Worry not. The moth shall come to the flame."

"Never mention fire to me again," warned the new Grump King.

DOOR EIGHTEEN

Edward was deep inside Bah Humbug so the children didn't hear his early morning snore, which was good news for Swish as she wasn't startled by it. She, Alf and Dylan had spent the night in the wooden tree house with the penguins. Swish had chosen to sleep there too because, despite everything he had done, she sensed Alf had a kind heart.

The tree house was a secret hiding place for any elves lucky enough to escape from Bah Humbug. The only way to reach it was by climbing a dangling rope ladder. The house was made from old fallen tree trunks and branches tied together with rope. It creaked, groaned and wobbled and there were cracks and some dangerous holes in the floor that were very scary because it was a long way down.

Hidden within a group of fir trees that kept it warm and sheltered, the tree house had somehow stood for many a Christmas. It was a brilliant look-out tower and there were some really cool and comfy hammocks to sleep in. Alf had let Dylan sleep on one on the promise that he didn't play his drum during the night. Thankfully, Dylan didn't let them down. But something he did let down was his hair. He'd taken off his Busby hat to reveal long glossy black hair that almost reached all the way to his bottom.

As the morning sun came up, Alf was on a rickety balcony overlooking the gloomy Bah Humbug fortress. He watched the gates hoping to see the polar bears emerge victorious with Teddy, Edward and the gifts. Swish sat on his shoulder and whispered something into his ear, "You get one wish with Swish!" But Alf wasn't paying attention because he was too busy thinking about the next bit of his plan.

In the igloo below, Jill was also thinking hard and fiddling frantically with her fringe. She had some ideas on how to rescue Edward and his bear, but wanted to see what was behind door eighteen. Skipping breakfast, she tugged the door open. Inside was a peculiar little snowman with a large black top hat. Deeply disappointed, she left it where it was and closed the door.

"Eh, what are you doing?" asked Carol.

"It was only a *stupid* snowman. How can that possibly help us to save Edward?"

Jack appeared from his box with an anxious face with droplets of sweat, "Oh my, I think I made a ghastly error. There's a Santa's clause that says once a door is opened you *must* take the gift out right away. It's bad luck to close the door again without removing the gift."

"*Bad luck*? Really Jack, what are you saying?" replied Jill, gobsmacked.

"Take it out. Quickly now, for the longer the snowman's in there. The worse the luck becomes."

"I do wonder about you sometimes Jack. Whose side are you *really* on?" snapped Jill. She opened the door again as quickly as she could and took out the snowman. She put him on the ground, where in a sparkle and a flash he grew bigger.

At first all seemed well. He was rather cheerful looking with a large top hat and a stripy red, gold and green scarf. The snowman had a crooked carrot for a nose and pebbles for eyes and a mouth. He had sticks for arms, gloves for hands and long feet on stick legs that were hidden by a plump body. He looked like he could topple over at any moment. The snowman burped long and loud and his stomach shrunk right down. There was a beastly smell of rotten carrots!

"Let's hope that's the bad luck over and done with," said Gordon.

"Bad luck? Who for? I feel a whole lot better after that," claimed the snowman.

Jill pressed the Shrink Me button. The snowman liked what he saw, "Ooh, look at all the wonderful snow. I'm truly in Heaven."

Dylan, Swish and the penguins scurried down from the tree house to greet him. "Wow, a real life snowman. That's outta sight," said Dylan, lifting his sunglasses and flicking back his long hair.

"Ooh, hair boy look at your drumsticks. I could really use those. Give them to me... *now*," demanded the snowman, moving towards the drummer boy.

"Hey, bug out dude. They're my jam sticks."

Jack did his best to stop the snowman, "Dylan's right. Pieces can't steal pieces from other pieces. That's a new rule. I just made it up!"

"Oooh, it's a puppet in a box," said the snowman. He wobbled awkwardly over to Jack and leant over him menacingly, "You want a *piece* of me?"

"Excuse me!" squealed Jack anxiously.

"Hang loose Man. Chill," urged Dylan.

"Ha! Look at me, I'm already chilled. I'm mostly made of snow," chuckled the snowman.

Alf had heard the jibber-jabbering and slipped down the ladder.

"What's going on here?" he asked.

"Ooh another little guy. Is this world full of them?" sniped the snowman. He took off his top hat and covered the jack-in-the-box with it.

Jack shrilled, "It's all gone dark. I hate the dark!" which was a strange thing for him to say, if you think about it.

Jill gasped, "I have to do something." She grabbed the elf-abet blocks and rolled them. They spelt, 'H, O, R, R, I, D'.

"Horrid? Oh no. This isn't good," she said.

The snowman nodded in agreement. He picked Jack up, shook him and hung him upside down. Jack dangled helplessly.

"Nobody tells Horrid what to do!"

Bits of mince pie fell out of Jack's box. Horrid scooped some up and stuffed it into his mouth. *Munch, crunch, munch!*

Jack had a strange view of the world but said, "You're not supposed to eat the food. That's a proper rule." He now had a fearful face.

Horrid forced Jack back in to his box, shut the lid and put him on the ground upside down. Horrid's tummy rumbled angrily. With a whiz and a bang the pebbles that made up Horrid's mouth fell to the ground and in their place appeared a mouth full of sharp icicle teeth. His carrot nose dropped off and an enormous Brussels sprout took its place. His eyes sunk into his head and glowed a fierce orange. Horrid's stick arms and legs turned into muscularly tree trunks. He grew taller, much, much taller. Horrid ROARED. It echoed all across Santarctica and frightened Swish and the robins away. The penguins wisely slid off down the hillside as fast as they could.

"He's turned abominable! Take cover," warned Alf.

It was complete chaos. Horrid thumped, bashed, stomped and smashed. The Santa Bravo Elite took a real beating. The steering wheel snapped and the screen on the Santa. Nav. broke. The driver's seat flew into the air, almost hitting the tree house. Horrid grabbed hold of Archie. He lifted the wooden Christmas tree into the air and swung it around his head. He snapped it in half and threw it to the ground. He pulled the handle from the gramophone and tossed it over the hill. He broke many of the records, ripped the lid off Jack's box then picked up Rocky, tore off his curved runners and threw them like javelins.

"No, not Rocky, please anyone but him," cried Nigel.

Horrid ignored his pleas for mercy. He grabbed hold of the igloo and stamped on it. Squelch! Last of all, he gathered up the elf-abet blocks and chucked them. They read, 'P, I, -, C, -, S'. Then, mercifully, Horrid stormed off, seeking something else to amuse him.

"Unreal. He was totally hacked off. What a bummer!" said Dylan, as he looked at all the terrible damage.

Shocked by all the destruction, everyone else stayed quiet, until they heard voices mumbling outside Bah Humbug.

Carol knew they were in more danger, "It's the grumps. They're coming. Quickly, we have to save what we can and get it into the tree house."

"She's right," said Jill.

"But I can't get up that tree," said Nigel. He was worrying terribly.

"That's right. He can't possibly get up there," said Gordon.

"One thing at a time... let's get going," urged Jill.

The children salvaged some scented candles, jars of gloopy green face cream, Clementine oranges, the elf-abet blocks, the Santarctica map, mistletoe and the snowball machine. Alf and the girls took it all up to the tree house. They also carried up the two halves of Archie, Jack with his broken lid, the fishing rod and the trampled igloo. They used the snowman's top hat to help carry the items up the ladder, including the last bits of the mince pie.

While they were doing this the grumps came ever closer. Luckily Rocky's legs still worked, but there was absolutely no chance he would be able to pull what was left of the sleigh anymore. Although Nigel could still ride him, the thought of doing so made him more nervous than ever.

Dylan did his bit to encourage Nigel, "Hey dude, its real heavy, but you need somewhere to crash and that's an awesome pad," he said, pointing to the tree house.

"But I'm afraid. I've got to go up the ladder on Rocky," said Nigel.

"Relax Man. You're uptight. We've got to split dude."

Jill called to them from the tree house, "Be brave. Find your courage again Nigel, Teddy did. Stop pussyfooting around. Rocky will keep you safe. Trust him. Climb. Do it now. The grumps are almost at the top of the hill."

Knowing he had no choice, Nigel took a deep breath and said, "Rocky on." It transported him on to the horse. Dylan took one of his drumsticks and gently tapped Rocky's rear. "Trot on!" he said. Nigel leant forward and wrapped his arms around Rocky's neck as he started to climb the ladder. Watching his friend safely reach the tree house, Gordon nervously followed him. One rung at a time, their worst fears had been conquered and they were safe.

Carol was thrilled, "I'm so proud of you guys. You really did it."

Dylan was the last to reach the tree house. He frantically pulled up the ladder, just as the first of the grumps arrived, followed by many more of the creepy little creatures. They clambered over the broken remains of the Santa Bravo Elite and celebrated by chanting the Grump Grumble. As they sang, the fortress grew a little bigger. The song had a message for the children, "I'm happy being a grump. I'm happy having the hump. We don't like Christmas, not one bit. Santa's stupid sleigh lies in pieces here today. We don't like Christmas not one bit. Can you hear us sing, Edward's our new king! We don't like Christmas, not one bit. And when Carol comes back down, we're going to grab her crown. We don't like Christmas, not one bit. There's no..."

Nigel had seen and heard enough. Suddenly and most unexpectedly, he grabbed the snowball machine. He set the dial to Rapid Fire Super Sized Snowballs. He began firing at the grumps with a whoosh, splat and kerpow!

"Nigel, what are you doing?" asked Gordon. "It'll make them meaner and greener."

"I don't care. I'm not afraid anymore. If we're going down, let's go down fighting."

Nigel kept snow-balling the grumps. He zapped too many to count, causing them to fall back down the hill to Bah Humbug. It was quite a sight. "Look at those grumps go!" he cried. It probably wasn't the wisest move ever, but it put smiles back on their faces. Everyone had a go on the snowball machine until the very last grump disappeared out of sight.

"I'm glad we're all safe, but where's Swish?" asked Alf, once things had settled down.

"All that noise must have scared her away, poor thing. I hope she's okay. I'm never closing a door on a gift again," said Jill glumly.

"Don't worry, I've a feeling she'll be back soon," said Carol, putting her arm around Jill and giving her a sisterly hug.

When the night arrived the bruised and battered grumps kept their distance. All was silent under the spell-bindingly beautiful northern lights, which was perfect for Jill. It gave her time to think about what to do next.

DOOR NINETEEN

When December the nineteenth arrived it was obvious to the children that they were in a very sticky spot. Although Archie was broken in two, remarkably, the few remaining unopened doors had somehow stayed shut. Door nineteen had already been opened by the grumps during their raid on Conjuring Cottage. It should have held the letter to Santa. There were just four more doors to go until Christmas. Time was running out so they had to act fast. It was a good job that Jill had finished doing her thinking. She had a marvellous master plan and shared it with everyone, but only once she'd finished peeling the skin of a Clementine and eating the flesh.

Step one of the plan involved the penguins and their fishing rod. Dasher, Blitzen and Prancer dug a hole in the snow close to the gates of Bah Humbug. They'd hastily made a 'No Fishing Aloud' sign and stuck it next to the hole.

Prancer dangled the fishing rod in the hole while the other penguins gathered about it, flapping their flippers in excitement.

"It's a whopper! What a fish!" cried Blitzen.

Dasher agreed, "It's got to be the biggest one yet."

The kerfuffle got the attention of the guards on the gate.

"I didn't think they could fish there," said Bandit.

Jasper replied, "I didn't think there were any fish there."

"What should we do?"

"I don't know Bandit. Fishing penguins ain't in the rule book neither."

"You're right. It isn't is it?"

"I like a bit of fishing," said Bandit.

"Me too, but I don't eat the fish... I only like sprouts... of course."

"Can I tell you something Bandit?" said Jasper. He whispered, "I actually don't much like sprouts."

"Me neither. Shall we go and take a look?"

"Yeah Bandit. It'll only take a minute. No one will know, will they?"

"Yeah. Let's do that."

So Bandit and Jasper waddled over to the excited penguins, leaving the Bah Humbug gates unguarded. Carol, Jill and Gordon took their chance. They were made up to look just like grumps. Each child had tied several Christmas jumpers about themselves, which had been soaked in the gloopy green face mask. They also wore it in their hair, face and hands. Their eyes were disguised with round pieces of the orange Clementine peel with holes cut out in the middle, stuck on with the gooey-ear candle wax.

It was extremely yucky but it worked. To complete the disguise they shuffled along on their knees. It was slow going, but they looked every inch like grumps, well good enough to fool a grump. Gordon carried all the items needed for the mission in the snowman's upturned top hat. Alf, pretending to be their prisoner, was not disguised as a grump.

Together, they sneaked through the gate and into Bah Humbug while the guards were distracted by the fishing penguins.

"What's all this?" asked Bandit.

"We're fishing," said Dasher.

"What you caught?" asked Jasper.

"A couple of whoppers."

Bandit was getting suspicious, "Where are they then?" he asked.

"We put them back again," claimed Prancer.

"But we didn't think there were any fish here... did we Bandit?"

"There might be Jasper. Look, the sign says, 'No Fishing Aloud'."

"It means you can fish here, but quietly," said Prancer, "otherwise you'll scare the fish away."

"Really! So where are the fish?" asked Jasper.

"Yeah, and I don't see no water either," said Bandit.

"That's because you've been fished in!" said Dasher. The penguins dropped the rod and quickly slid away, leaving the guards bemused.

"Those penguins are so stupid. What do they mean, 'fished in'?" asked Bandit.

"They're so dumb," replied Jasper.

"Hey look Jasper, they only went and left the rod behind. Fancy a go?"

"Yeah. We'll show them. But keep quiet we don't want to scare the fish away now do we?"

They dangled the rod in the hole with no water.

"Nothing... diddly-squat," said Bandit after a few minutes.
"That's because we haven't got any bait, stupid."
"Do fish like sprouts?" Bandit asked.
"I do wonder about you sometimes, *I really do*."

***

Inside Bah Humbug Alf led the disguised children through the tunnels. The further they went in the darker and smellier it got. Alf knew every inch of the way and whenever they met a grump, he told the children what to do and say.

Jill put on a gruff voice, "Hello grumpy. We got Alf... the stupid Master Elf. Thinks he can outsmart us grumps. No chance. We're taking him to the General."

The plan seemed to be working, until they got close to the cells.
One grump suggested, "Put that scoundrel in here with the others. We've got some Sprout Supreme. It'll do him good and proper."
Carol put on her grumpiest voice, "You can have your fun with him later. We got business with General Grump with this one."
"But we was told not to let anyone see the General today. He's busy with the new king, ain't he Oscar?"
"Yep! Hey if it ain't little Lord Alfie. Come back have you? An elf called Alf. Alf the Elf. Alfie the Elfie sitting on a shelfie."
"That's enough of that," said Gordon, forgetting to put on a grumpy voice.
"Hey, what is this? Do I know you? What's in that hat?" asked Oscar.
"It's a load of fresh sprouts... wonderful sprouts," claimed Carol. She clicked her fingers, lighting the Soggy Sprout Farts candle.
"Let me see then," asked the grump.
With their disguise under threat, Jill tried to distract the guards, "Hey Oscar, don't you remember me?"
"What? No, who are you?"
"Oscar, how could you forget me? I'm dismayed."

"Dismayed?" asked Oscar. "Ah yeah, I remember. Dismayed, you ain't changed much. Just a bit squidgier, that's all."

"Squidgier, am I?" asked Jill with her pride dented.

The lit Soggy Sprout Farts candle inside the top hat was busy making a revolting stinky stench.

"Yep and you smell delicious. I'll be waiting for you once you're done with the General," said the grump, winking, "Say hello to the bear for me, If he can still hear... they were going to take his good ear off last I knew."

Alf and the children went further into the fortress, deceiving many a grump on the way. Eventually they reached the main chamber. There were many grumps huddled about the chest and throne, mumbling about victory and the end of Christmas forever. They had laid Teddy on top of the chest and covered him in cold soggy sprouts. He was a sticky green mess.

Jill cried out in her best grumpy grump voice, "Hey, we got the master of the elves."

Every grump in the chamber stopped what they were doing to gawp at her.

"What's this?" said General Grump, "Ah, Alf you've come back. So... now you've led Edward into our trap I suppose you think I'll give the order to release your friends, do you?"

"You promised me. I did all you asked, now let my people go," demanded Alf.

"So I did Alf... but things have changed. Look, we have a new king. Let's hear what he has to say about this."

A hush fell over the chamber. The crowd of grumps shuffled about to reveal the new Grump King. They loyally followed him over to the unexpected visitors. Teddy sat up on the chest with green gunk dripping off his nose.

The Grump King spoke, "It's you Alf! What are you doing here? I don't trust you."

The children were horrified by Edward's appearance. There was so little left of the old Edward. It was a good thing that the cat had their tongue as they didn't want to give the game away.

"Is that you Buddy? What have they done to you?" asked Alf.

"I'm *not* your buddy and this was my choice."

The Grump King shuffled over to Jill, Carol and Gordon. He was suspicious of the daringly disguised children. He eyed them up and down, stroking the AAA medallion hanging around his neck. General Grump had not long given it to him, believing it held a special power.

"Listen carefully to me," said the Grump King, "I know your game. You are heroes for bringing this dumb dimwit to me. Nobody messes with the Grump King. I'm going to teach this elf a lesson he'll never, *ever*, forget."

"*Dumb dimwit*? The kid's a natural. I like it," said General Grump.

The other grumps liked it too and chanted, "Grump King! Grump King! Grump King!"

"This way, I know just what to do with you," said the new Grump King.

"Throw him in the pit with the bears? *Do it*!" urged General Grump.

"Patience General! Let's have some fun... Oh Alf, I remember how much you hated being trapped inside the Advent calendar. You *really* hated it, didn't you?"

"*I did*? I did!" mumbled Alf.

"You have a terrible fear of small dark places, don't you Alf?" he said, grabbing Alf roughly and dragging him over to the wooden chest. Teddy was still sat on it, trying to shake off the green sprout goo.

"Oh, it's you, Alf. The little liar! You didn't tell Edward we were going on the picnic, did you?" snarled Teddy.

"It was just a picnic Teddy."

"*Just a picnic*, you ruined it," said Teddy.

"Well now we get our revenge. In to the chest with you," said the Grump King.

Accidentally on purpose, Teddy slid off the chest leaving a trail of green gunk behind him. He landed right next to the trap door lever.

"*Please* don't put me in the chest, anything but that," pleaded Alf, seemingly struggling to get away.

"How perfectly mean!" rejoiced General Grump.

The Grump King took off the medallion and used it as a key to open the chest. Its heavy top rolled back with a clump. Inside the chest were Archie's stolen gifts - Santa's sack, the Christmas pudding and the letter to Santa. "Best place for them," said the Grump King. He glanced over to the three disguised children and said, "And you, grump heroes, you brought this fool to me. You deserve a reward. Come here... you can have the pleasure of locking him in the chest."

The children began shuffling over to the chest, but General Grump cried, "HALT!" He had spotted something out of order. Too much shuffling had caused the green face mask on the back of Carol's crown to fall away. The game was up as the shiny gold paper was there for all to see. "You're not grumps," fumed General Grump, "And that's the Coronation Crown on your head. It doesn't belong to you. It belongs to the King of the Grumps and will make him our king forever."

The Grump King rushed over to Carol, "That crown belongs to me. Give me back what's rightfully mine." As he reached for the crown, Carol swiftly and skilfully took the sprig of mistletoe from the top hat, held it over the king's head and kissed him on the lips, which wasn't at all easy for her because of how Edward looked right then.

"NO!" cried General Grump, "Not the cursed mistletoe!"

Suddenly, a shimmering purple haze swamped the Grump King. He started to become less grumpy. His big droopy nose began to shrink, the orange glow in his eyes dwindled, his shiny white teeth grew back, his pot belly disappeared, his skin returned to its usual colour, he went back to his normal height, and, last of all, the long curly white hair had totally vanished from his chin. He was Edward once more. Jill and Carol shrieked with joy, while Alf punched the air with glee.

"Imposters. GET THEM!" fumed General Grump.

At that very moment, Teddy reached for the trap door lever. Pulling with all his might the lever moved and the trap door swung open.

"Mummy Bear, Daddy Bear. I'm sleepy," cried Teddy.

There was a mighty growl. The grumps froze in fear as the massive bears scrambled out of the pit and bounded over to Teddy. The grumps panicked and began to scatter in all directions with some bumping into each other and tumbling over like skittles.

"Clever Teddy, you saved us... but you're all sticky and green," said Mummy Bear.

"Shall we carry you off to bed?" asked Daddy Bear.

"Not yet, I'm not *really* sleepy. I was just pretending, not lying."

"Oh Edward, I thought we'd lost you forever," said Jill.

"No Jill... I was also pretending... but *not* lying. You said it was okay to pretend. It was Carol's big eyelashes that gave her away. I saw them behind the orange peel."

Carol blushed under the gloopy green face mask and fluttered her eyelashes in celebration.

"You two had me going there," said Alf. "I was shaking in my boots. I thought I was going in the chest with the gifts. Let's grab them and get out of this stinky dump."

The polar bears raced about the chamber causing the rest of the grumps to flee, but General Grump stood his ground, "This isn't over, I promise you," he claimed defiantly.

"Shush, grump face. I'm thinking about what we should do with you," said Jill, fiddling with her fringe.

"Let's tie *him* to the throne," suggested Edward.

So that's what they did. Jill placed a pair of scented candles on the chest, labelled Happy Smiley Faces. She nodded to Edward, who clicked his fingers and lit the candles. For the first time in forever, General Grump's down-turned mouth turned upwards. He smiled in the face of defeat.

"We're not done yet," said Carol. "Give him some Christmas pudding. It's packed with Christmas spirit."

Edward broke off a small piece of the Christmas pudding. "Eat!" he said. General Grump already had a beaming smile, so it was easy for Edward to push the pudding into his mouth.

The mysterious purple haze reappeared around General Grump. His nose shrunk. His teeth grew back. He was no longer green and his eyes no longer glowed orange. General Grump had turned back into a real boy. He was a ragged one, with tangled orangey-brown hair and a turned-up nose.

"Look what you've done to me. I was happy being a grump. I was happy having the hump. I don't like Christmas, not one bit."

"This boy's so naughty," said Jill, shaking her head, "Okay, once we're done with him let's light more candles and sprinkle bits of the pudding into every sprout pot we can find."

"I demand you untie me. This isn't fair, not one bit," said the boy, struggling to break free.

Jill took the elf-abet blocks out of the hat.

"Let's see what the blocks have to say about that shall we." She tumbled the blocks. They read, 'V, I, C, T, O, R'.

"There, I knew it! We win and you lose," claimed Gordon, with one eye on the tasty Christmas pudding.

"No, it doesn't mean that," said Carol, "His name is Victor, isn't it?"

"Yes. I'm Victor," admitted the boy.

"Victor?" said Edward.

"And Christmas isn't about winners or losers," said Carol, "To win In this game we have to let him go."

It was the right thing to do so they untied him. The boy leapt from the throne, "Pah," he mumbled, before quickly grabbing the king's medallion out of the chest's lock. "And this belongs to me," he said, then scampered off towards one of the tunnels, calling behind him, "This isn't over yet... and Edward when you said you didn't believe in Father Christmas. You lied. Didn't you?"

"He's another lost boy," said Carol, "Terribly lost."

***

The cell guards watched their fellow grumps waddle by as quickly as their legs would allow.

"What's happening?" asked Oscar.

"Oscar, it's terrible. They're making us smile by force feeding us Christmas pudding."

"Christmas pudding? I thought that was banned."

"It is banned."

"So why are they eating it?" asked Oscar.

"Beats me! Give me Sprout Supreme any day."

At which point Alf returned to the elves cells with The Three Bears beside him.

"I told you I'd be back," said Daddy Bear, beginning to pull some cell bars apart.

"Fine, but you won't find Goldilocks here," said Oscar.

"Or Red Riding Hood," said another grump.

"You bozo! We've been through that already. I give up!" sighed Oscar.

"Let my brother elves go," demanded Alf.

"Here... take the keys," said Oscar.

"What about the sisters... we're the forgotten elves," said one of the jailed girl elves.

"So much for equality!" said another.

"Alright, and my sisters," added Alf.

The guards opened the rest of the cell doors, freeing all the thankful elves.

***

Beyond the gates to Bah Humbug, Dylan and Nigel waited. Dylan was ready to sound the alarm if he spotted Horrid the abominable snowman returning, by banging his drum as loudly as he could. Nigel manned the snowball machine. His job was to stop any grumps from escaping.

As grumps began to flee the fortress and make for the gates, Nigel fired the snowball machine. He aced it! Hitting one grump after another and knocking them off their feet. But, there was something more, Nigel was stunned as one by one the snowballed grumps turned back into elves.

"I'm free! I'm an elf again," cried Bandit joyfully.

"The curse has been broken!" celebrated Jasper.

"Hey, man! That's boss!" said Dylan, bashing out a celebratory drum roll, which probably wasn't the wisest thing to do because of Swish.

And so it was that every grump that ever there was turned back into the elf they once were. The gate guards, Bandit and Jasper, had been amongst the last to do so.

They were so excited they ran over to the penguins and embraced them. Prancer spun about and slipped on to his bottom.

"Not again!" said Prancer with a smile.

The whole gang soon emerged from the fortress. The children could finally remove the orange peel from their eyes and see properly again. They made their way to the gate holding the recovered stolen gifts, with Teddy riding proudly on Daddy Bear's back. In celebration, the air was suddenly filled with hundreds of robins, including Edward's. He twiddled his thumbs and Peter flew down and landed on to his shoulder.

"Thank you Peter... my happy childhood memories that you captured helped me in my darkest moments as a grump. When I twiddled my thumbs I thought of my parents and how much they loved me... and loved Christmas."

They all watched as snow fell upon Bah Humbug for the first time in many a Christmas, so long in fact that nobody could remember the last time it happened.

***

In the jubilation that followed, the children had quite forgotten about the Horrid destruction to the Santa Bravo Elite, Archie and many of the gifts. They made their way back up to the tree house, but, sadly, as they feared, everything was still in pieces.

Jack had already popped up and had an emoji face with a head bandage, "So you're back then Edward. Well done old chap. Hollow victory though, unless of course you were listening properly. I said right at the start that you needed to listen very carefully but did you?"

"Listen?" asked Edward, looking about in utter disbelief at all the carnage.

Jill put a finger to her lips, "SHUSH everyone! I'm trying to listen."

Everyone fell silent. It was the kind of hush only possible in the wild open spaces of Santarctica. Alf put an end to it with a sprightly claim, "That's it! You get one wish with Swish! I heard her say it, I remember now," he cried excitedly and danced a little jig.

So it was that Christmas miracle number three happened. Calmed by the silence, Swish returned right on cue. She flew over to Alf and kissed his cheek.

"Alf and Swish sitting in a tree..." sang Edward, and everyone joined in with, "K, I, S, S, I, N, G."

"Peace and love Man," beamed Dylan.

Everyone giggled.

"If there's only one wish?" began Nigel, "Can't we just wish for many wishes?"

"Bad form," said Jack firmly, "We mustn't be greedy. Be careful what you wish for or all the good that has been done could be undone."

"I just wish you'd explained all the rules properly... then we wouldn't be in this trouble," said Jill without thinking, which was a rare thing in itself.

"You get one wish with Swish!" confirmed the fairy. Her words made Jill's wish come true, right there and then.

"No wait," urged Edward, but it was already too late.

"There's no turning back now!" said Jack. He slipped into his box, pleasantly surprised to find its lid was back on, and working just fine.

In a sparkle and a flash the Santa Bravo Elite was as good as new again. Archie was no longer broken in two, Rocky's runners were repaired and the gramophone and records fixed. It seemed Jill had made the perfect wish, as now she would have known not to leave the snowman behind door eighteen for even one second after she'd opened it, which meant the snowman never ate the pie, turned abominable, and broke Archie, the sleigh and so on.

At that point, Horrid appeared at the top of the hill, but thanks to Jill's wish Horrid no longer lived up to his name. He was gentle and not in the least abominable. He was back to his true self and without a trace of the bad luck caused by Jill.

"I beg your pardon," said the snowman politely, "But I appear to have misplaced my topper. Have you by chance seen it?"

"Yes Horrid, we have it," said Jill, "And it was so very useful too, thank you."

"Horrid? Me? Why young lady you are most mistaken. My name is Horace."

"Hello Horace, I'm Edward. I don't believe we've had the pleasure."

"Good day Edward," said the snowman bowing awkwardly as though on stilts.

Jack came back out of his box. He now had a relieved emoji face. He was holding the largely uneaten mince pie, "Behold... I still have it. Horace didn't turn bad so he didn't turn me on my head, shake the pie out and eat it!" he cried.

But Horace said, "I say, is that a mince pie? I do love a mince pie. May I?"

"NO!" cried everyone, scaring Swish away again.

"Why?" he asked, "Will it make me go green like some of you?"

The children giggled and Jill said, "We don't normally look this bad, I promise."

Relieved to have the igloo back in one piece, the children shed their disguise and washed off the gloopy green face mask. They were squeaky clean and happy to be themselves again.

DOOR TWENTY

In the igloo, Edward may have been cured of his grumpiness, but he still needed his forty winks. Up in the tree house, his mighty snore caught Dylan and Horace by surprise. Swish though was expecting it, so, for once, she found the courage to stay put. That was until Dylan fell off his hammock with a THUMP. It shook the creaky floor, causing Alf to giggle and scaring Swish away.

Edward had been up all night studying the map of Santarctica closely. He was holding the map when Teddy pressed the igloo's Shrink Me button, and had it in his hands when everyone gathered to see what was inside door twenty.

"We're still in a fix," said Edward, pointing in turn to various places on the map, "It's much too far for Rocky to get us from here to Tinsel Town in time for Christmas... and the elves don't even have the letters to Santa yet."

Jack came out of his box. He had a thinking face, "It's true. You're in a spot of bother and we have the pesky grumps to thank for that... their shenanigans slowed us right down."

"Well let's just open door twenty Edward," said Jill. She was still being bossy! "But please make sure you take out what's inside before you close it. We don't want to make that mistake again."

"Don't worry. I've a good feeling about this one," said Carol.

Edward happily opened the door. He pulled out a little red-nosed reindeer and put it down. In a sparkle and a flash Rudolph grew bigger. Carol and her singers burst into song, "Rudolph the red nosed reindeer had a very shiny nose. And if you ever saw it, you would surely say it... glows?"

Rudolph twitched his nose, "Howdy folks. I'm Rudolph, but you already know that don't you for I'm the most famous reindeer of all! I'm the history maker, celebrity, a superstar because of my nose. See how it glows."

Alas, Rudolph's nose didn't glow, not one bit.

"It's all very fabulous, but there's a teeny-tiny problem here, just a little detail," said Jack.

"What's up little guy?" asked Rudolph.

"You still look... very majestic," said Jill.

"And your antlers are stunning," added Edward.

"And your eyes are huge," said Carol uneasily.

"It's my nose, *isn't it*? It's not glowing," said Rudolph.

He went cross-eyed trying to see it for himself, "Ooh, it means I've got the heebee-jeebies. Something must have happened to Santa. We have to get to Tinsel Town and in double-quick time."

"But even if Rocky did his best, we can't make it there in time. It's impossible," said Edward.

"Ha, well my nose doesn't glow, but I can still fly. Let's ride shotgun. Rein me up. Rocky and I can pull the sleigh together."

Quick as could be, Edward, Jill, Archie and all the pieces were aboard the Santa Bravo Elite. It was a squeeze but they'd even packed Teddy's picnic basket too.

"This time I *will* hold on to my hat," promised Alf.

"No need. Just press the weather deflector button. It's a force field that keeps out all the wind, rain and snow. It's the blue button right under the steering wheel," explained Rudolph.

"Oh, I wondered what that was for," said Edward.

"It's Santa's favourite gadget on the sleigh! He doesn't like getting his beard wet!" chuckled Rudolph.

Now that everyone and everything was on board, the adventure could continue. Sadly, there was no space left on the sleigh for all the rescued elves, the penguins and the polar bears. It was the second sad goodbye, but the elves made a promise to see them all again in Tinsel Town.

"We'll find a way. It's what elves do," said Bandit.

"Exactly that. We'll see you there," added Jasper.

Dasher winked at the two elves, "And we'll bring the fishing rod."

"Goodbye son," said Daddy Bear.

"Take good care of that bear Edward," pleaded Mummy Bear.

"I will... and I'll do it *just right*, like your porridge!"

Edward gave the command, "Dash on Rudolph, dash on Rocky. Dash away, dash away!"

Rudolph clicked his hooves and the Santa Bravo Elite took to the skies.

Beneath them the elves, penguins and polar bears waved and cheered. Edward pressed the weather deflector button and an invisible shield covered them. They soared upwards leaving the newly snow covered fortress of Bah Humbug behind.

Ahead was Tinsel Town in all its sparkling glory. It was a magical flight that carried them all the way to their destination just as the northern lights were appearing. When they got closer they saw unicorns guarding the town and the forest of candy cane trees. A glorious gold bow looped over a grand arch. It was the majestic entrance to Tinsel Town.

As the sleigh came in to land they saw cottages huddled together with lights at the windows and smoke from the chimneys. There was an enormous red, gold and green building in the shape of a pile of wrapped presents stacked higgledy-piggledy on top of each other. On top of the house of gifts was a dazzling bright light, just like a star that had fallen from Heaven. The building had grand windows with shutters and several large red doors. There was a fairground with carousel rides, a ferris wheel, a roller-coaster, dodgems, and a floodlit sports field. But the rides and field were all deserted.

On top of a hill stood a cabin with gold flashing letters upon its roof that read, 'GROTTO'. A long silver slide led from the grotto down the hill towards a large heart-shape sculpture made of candy canes. Nearby was a collection of old-fashioned red mail boxes.

The Santa Bravo Elite's runway was lit with fairy lights and baubles. Rudolph landed the sleigh smoothly and brought it to a graceful halt. Edward turned off the weather deflector shield. All was eerily quiet in Tinsel Town. Not a single elf was there to greet them and there was absolutely no sign of Santa Claus. This was not what they had expected, not one bit.

"It's much worse than I feared. Tinsel Town has lost its sparkle," said Rudolph.

"Where are all my brothers and sisters?" asked Alf, "They must be in the workshop."

Everyone climbed out of the sleigh and began to gather up the gifts. As Alf picked up the letter to Santa, Jill tried to gather up the elf-abet blocks. They slipped from her fingers, fell to the floor and spelt, 'D, I, S, M, A, Y'. "Dismay?" she said, "Not *more* trouble, surely."

"I had a horrible feeling something like this might happen," said Carol.

"*Dismay*? I say we hang tough!" said Dylan. He picked up Jack and placed him and his box on top of his drum.

"I'm cool with this, but absolutely no jamming Man, understood?" said Jack.

Teddy took Edward by the hand. He whispered, "I think the blocks said 'dismay' because of what you said at Bah Humbug about not believing in Father Christmas."

"You're very wise Teddy, but I did what I had to do. I don't regret it. Not one bit." Edward could see the loose stuffing in Teddy's better ear. It reminded him that it had been a close call, but he still believed he'd done the right thing in saving Teddy.

***

Alf led them to one of the shiny red doors in the enormous and colourful gift-wrapped building. There was a key pad security entry system. He tapped in the numbers two, zero, one, two. The door pinged and slowly opened into complete darkness. Alf clicked his fingers and scented candles lit up the room. Beneath the candles was a reception desk with a sign that read, 'The Most Wonderful Time of the Year'. Upon it were miniature models of Santa, penguins, reindeer and snowmen. On the wall behind the desk were framed pictures of previous winners of the prestigious 'Tinsel Town Elf of the Year' award.

"Most peculiar... this way," said Alf.

He led them through another door to yet more darkness, apart from a light in the distance. Alf clicked his fingers. Many ceiling lights flickered into life, revealing a gigantic room with row after row of tall empty shelving. Here and there were posters celebrating the joy of giving at Christmas and pictures of happy children opening gifts on Christmas morning. Several large speakers also hung from the walls. There was a huge digital clock counting down the days, hours, minutes and seconds to Christmas Day.

One wall was completely covered with a massive TV screen displaying a map of the world. Every country on it had little boxes with numbers that all showed *zero*. In the top corner of the map were the words Grand Total, which was also set to zero. Below the map were units packed with controllers, buttons and levers.

"Where *is* everyone?" asked Alf.

They all went further into the elves workshop and felt dwarfed by its giganticness. Their footsteps echoed as they passed rows of desks with turned-off laptops and tablets. There was a workers canteen with pulled down shutters. Next to it was a door headed, 'THE BOSS!'

"In here," said Alf.

It was a small humdrum room for a boss. There was a wobbly round table with a scented candle and several simple chairs. Alf clicked his fingers and the room lit up with a strong scent of Scottish shortbread. There were more empty shelves, coat hooks and a chart on the wall headed, 'My Big Day' with new items added including, Kick Some Butt, Happy Reunion and Twist in the Tale. There was another list headed Archie's Gifts. It began with, 1. Jack-in-the-box. 2. Santa Sweet. 3. Robin. 4. Christmas Fairy... and so on. The last entry read 22. Santa's Sack. Numbers 21, 23 and 24 were left blank. In one corner was an old friend - a floral winged-back armchair. There was a food bowl near it, marked Kat.

The bosses room had another door. It was red with a wonky number 25 on it and another sign, 'No Toys Allowed'.

They were amazed to see so many of Aphrodite's things. Edward asked, "Does Aphrodite work here? Is she the boss?"

"Well it does say 'The Boss' on the door," replied Alf.

"So this is where she went to every day," said Gordon.

"But how?" asked Edward, puzzled. "Conjuring Cottage is too far away."

"Maybe all isn't as it seems," suggested Carol.

"You can leave the gifts in here, but I'm definitely *not* going on any shelf. Everything will be perfectly safe," said Alf.

They placed Archie the Advent Calendar in a corner with Santa's sack. On the table they put the gramophone and records, Teddy's picnic basket, the igloo, elf-abet blocks, and what was left of the Christmas pudding. Alf kept the letter to Santa firmly in his hand and Dylan left Jack and his box safely on his drum.

"What's next?" asked Edward.

"They must be in the games room. Let's go," said Alf.

The children, Dylan, Horace, Rocky and Swish followed Alf to the back of the workshop. Alf pushed open large double doors to reveal hundreds of glum looking elves sitting idly playing board games and cards. The elves stopped what they were doing and eyed-up the visitors. "Brothers, sisters I'm back and with awesome news. We've cured Christmas of the grumps and freed the elves from Bah Humbug. They're on their way home. And I have in my hand the letter to Santa. Our work can begin."

Yet there was no applause or excited fanfare. Instead a solitary elf got up and walked slowly towards Alf.

"We're in dismay," said the elf quietly. "It's Father Christmas. *He's gone*. He vanished three days ago right before our eyes. We've no idea where he is. I'm afraid Christmas is cancelled *forever*."

"We know why, don't we? Someone broke the rules," said Jack. "And there's only one rule to Archie's Advent Adventure that could cause such a terrible thing. Someone has said what they absolutely should not about you know who and for a third time."

Edward bravely confessed, "It was me. I said it, but I had no choice. General Grump made me do it. He was going to pull off Teddy's good ear."

"I'm really sorry Edward," said Teddy, squeezing Edward's hand tightly.

The solitary elf spoke, "So you're Edward? The one everyone in Tinsel Town has been talking about. Yet you did *that*? We were obviously wrong about you. How disappointing." He tutted and began to make his way back to his seat.

"Poppycock," said Alf, "Without Edward, we'd still have the Christmas grumps. Because of him our fellow elves are free. He's a hero and my buddy!"

"And mine," said Carol.

"And he's my brother... and I'm proud of him!" said Jill.

DOOR TWENTY-ONE

The children didn't much like what some of the elves thought about Edward, so they spent the night in the igloo. Edward was still unable to sleep without his forty winks and woke them with his usual loud snore.

Bright and early, Alf led everyone back to the workshop, into the boss' office and closed the door. It was a real squeeze with them all in one small room, so it quickly warmed up. Horace got hotter and hotter. He complained, "I'm afraid I'll melt if you don't proceed quickly."

"We can't have that... come on... I'm *soooo* excited to see what's behind the door. I've a feeling it'll put the sparkle back into Tinsel Town," said Carol.

"Yes, let's do it," said Edward. He opened door twenty-one. Inside was a Christmas Angel. Edward took her out and showed everyone. She had long blonde hair and was wearing a graceful white satin dress with a tiara. Edward was about to put the angel down when it vanished. There was a playful 'rat-a-tat-tat' on the office door. As Jill opened it, Edward ducked behind her. Waiting by the door was the Christmas Angel.

"Hello my darlings. It's my *Big Day*. Hurrah! Have you missed me? It's so wonderful to see you all again," said Aphrodite joyfully. She had a beaming smile and was wearing a glamorous white gown, a long blonde wig and a tiara.

The children were speechless.

"What's up, Kat got your tongue?"

Kat was at her feet, next to Aphrodite's familiar reindeer-faced slippers.

"Aphrodite, it's you and you look *so* beautiful," said Jill.

"Beautiful me? Why I'm so much more than that. I'm absolutely fabulous!" replied Aphrodite. In celebration, she and Kat did a delightful little twirl, revealing a pair of real angel wings.

"You're a real angel! Awesome," said Edward.

"I just knew we'd see you again," added Carol, fiddling with the paper crown still stuck firmly on her head.

Once Aphrodite squeezed into her office, Swish flew about her wings, sniffing and stroking them. The elf-abet blocks were on Aphrodite's desk. Accidentally-on-purpose, her angel wings brushed against them. They tumbled and spelt, 'C, I, R, C, L, - '.

"Oh a circle," said Aphrodite, "What comes around goes around. I trust you are having an adventure to remember children? Look at your amazing new friends... Horace and Dylan, oh there are my sunglasses. Spectacular!"

"It's been a gas! And the shades are fab!" said Dylan.

"I am most humbled," nodded Horace, still feeling the heat and starting to drip. Wisely, he decided to stand by the door where it was cooler.

"Oh, and I hear you defeated the grumps. Stupendous work team! And look Archie is safe and well, bless him." She kissed the star on top of Archie then wrote 'Christmas Angel' against number 21 on the list of Archie's gifts using a red magic marker that hung on a piece of tinsel beside it.

Jack was already out of his box. He had a big grinning face, "Aphrodite, it's a joy to see you, of course, but I'm afraid there's a bit of a problem. You see Edward said the thing that mustn't be said about you know who for the third time, so it would appear that Christmas is cancelled."

"Christmas is cancelled, *gobbledygook*? Everything is perfectly marvellous! We've work to do. Alf, did you deliver the letter to Santa?"

"No Aphrodite. It's still here on your desk."

"Master Elf, you're neglecting your duties. Get with it!" urged Aphrodite.

"So I'm still Master Elf am I, despite everything?"

"Why of course. You're an extraordinary elf who most certainly should not be sat on a shelf. If anyone can help us to rediscover the Christmas Spirit it's you... all of you in fact. You are the baubles on my tree and the twinkle in my fairy lights. I'd be lost without you," said Aphrodite. She began to sing, "O come all ye faithful, joyful and triumphant. O come ye, O come ye to... to... to."

Everyone giggled.

"That's the spirit!" she said, gleefully rubbing her hands together. She led them all to the giant electronic map of the world. Next to the control units was a special slot for Archie's letter to Santa, "Mm, it's a deli-*cat* task, so who should I pick to mail the letter to Santa?"

All the children raised their hands, but Kat flapped her ears, curled her tail and meowed.

"*Purr*-fect," said Aphrodite. "We need to *cat*-ch up, so you'll do just fine."

Kat took the letter in her mouth, stretched up to the slot and put it in. She used the tip of her nose to push the letter all the way inside.

"You really are the cat's whiskers, Kat," said Aphrodite. She rewarded Kat by picking her up and giving her sloppy kitty kisses. Kat wriggled free, leapt to the ground and walked off with a swagger, just like a model on the catwalk.

The children giggled.

The gigantic world map blinked and flashed into life. Numbers lit up against all the main cities in the world - places like London, Paris and New York. There was a grand total at the top of the map that showed more than a billion and a much smaller number below that in red, which had just appeared.

"That's a whole lot of children and a whole lot of letters. It gets bigger every year. Those in red are on the naughty list," said Alf.

"The *naughty* list," gasped Gordon.

"I wouldn't want to be on that," replied Nigel.

The laptops and tablets on the desks behind them sprang to life, beeping and playing the tune of, 'Santa Claus is coming to Town'. The Christmas music spread to the games room. The door opened and confused elves started to emerge.

"There you all are. Stupendous news! The children's letters to Santa have arrived. Get online and read those emails and social media posts. We're all running a bit late, so we mustn't dawdle," ordered Aphrodite.

"But didn't they tell you," said the 'unelected spokes-elf', "Christmas is cancelled. Santa disappeared."

"*Poppycock*! Look at me. I'm ready and you should be too. If we lost Santa, we can get him back again. We just need to rekindle the Christmas Spirit. Now, go to it or do I have to kick some butt with my reindeer slippers?" and by the serious look on her face, they knew she meant business.

As ordered, the elves *got to it*. They began logging-on to deal with the messages to Santa from children all over the world. As they read the messages, the grand total number on the world map started to go down.

"Oh, and we need to check the post boxes outside," said Alf. The children were curious and followed him. The red pillar boxes were jam-packed with letters and bundles of mail sacks were piled up against them. Alf took a letter out and read it, "Dear Santa, last week my uncle said you looked like a fat wrinkly old tomato! I told him off right there and then and he said 'sorry'. As I've been *soooo* good this year, could you please bring me..." But Alf stopped reading and put the letter back in its envelope, "Nope, us elves are sworn to secrecy on every child's Christmas wishes." Alf straightened his hat and said, "Now then, we could do with some help collecting up all these letters."

Just then something most unexpected arrived at the entrance to Tinsel Town. The rescued elves from Bah Humbug had built the most ingenious jingly-jangly travel machine in the world ever by far. They named it the Whatchamacallit.

The returning elves had recycled the Bah Humbug gates, sprout cauldrons, cell bars, lanterns, goblets, and the chain of jingle bells that had surrounded the fortress, and used Sprout Supreme as fuel. The inventive elves had re-imagined it all into something truly incredible. The humdinger of a flying apparatus looked a little like a giant metallic bumblebee and flew like one.

The magnificent musical Whatchamacallit had carried the elves and penguins all the way to Tinsel Town in record time.

After a joyous reunion with their fellow elves, they got to work enthusiastically emptying the mail boxes and dragging all the sacks into the workshop. As Master Elf, Alf had the job of opening Jill and Edward's personal letters to Santa.

He opened Jill's first. It read, "Dear Santa, I didn't mean to get angry with my brother or boss him about. This year has been the worst year ever by far in the whole world. Mother is always asking me to look after Edward and sometimes he's so annoying. I'm really sorry about Teddy's ear. Can you please fix it for him? Can you also find the Santa Sweet because we need it to save Christmas? Oh, and can you please get Aphrodite something special. She's truly an angel and really deserves it."

Alf then read Edward's letter, "Dear Santa, if you're real, you'll know why I have the Christmas grumps and why I said what I did about not believing. I don't really want anything new this year. All I want is to grow up fast. I also want a good night's sleep because it's making me tired. And can you fix Teddy's ear and get a new spring for Jack. I didn't mean to hurt him. Can I also ask you for something very special? I just want my Daddy back for Christmas. Mummy is sad and it won't be the same without him."

Alf was sworn to secrecy about the letters, but when he next saw Edward he gave him one almighty hug.

***

Later, as the sun went down Aphrodite went to a cupboard in the workshop reception area. She removed her blonde wig and tiara and put them inside, then took out her shaggy brown coat and clumpy boots. Edward and Jill were with her. "Well children, Kat and I have had an extremely wonderful and busy day," said Aphrodite. "I'm off now for a lovely warm bubble bath and some scrumptious hot chocolate. See you all bright and early tomorrow morning."

"But Conjuring Cottage is so far away. You can't possibly get there in time," argued Edward.

"Oh did I not tell you? Conjuring Cottage is just through the Lost Woods behind Santa's Grotto."

"Ugh, I don't understand. *What are you saying*?" asked Jill.

"Conjuring Cottage is part of Tinsel Town, how else could all the magic happen?"

"That's just ridiculous," chuckled Jill.

"What comes around goes around. You've been travelling in a circle. A ginormous one I admit, but a circle all the same."

"But we walked in the Lost Woods for absolutely ages... and every single path took us back to the cottage again," said Jill.

"That would be right because Conjuring Cottage knows best. It let the light guide you."

"The light?" asked Edward.

"The really bright one on top of the elves workshop, it's the Christmas Spirit. You can see it all the way from the Lost Woods. Come now Kat, my bath will be getting cold and the bubbles will be all a-popping."

She picked up Kat and left the workshop. The children were very tempted to follow her, but didn't because Alf needed their help with the letters.

DOOR TWENTY-TWO

Door twenty-two on Archie had been opened days ago by the grumps. It would have held Santa's sack. It was the very sack the grumps used to capture Edward, but now awaited the Christmas presents for every child in the world. Wow! That's a tremendously gigantically enormous number of presents indeed.

The elves were up with the morning sun. They chuckled when they heard Edward's loud snore. In a strange sort of way it helped them to forgive him for saying that thing he wasn't supposed to say about Santa. When Aphrodite arrived, the elves had already *got to it* crafting wonderful toys of every kind imaginable.

It got a bit messy at times, especially when some of the elves flicked paint from their brushes to make freckles on dolls faces. It left a few elves with freckles that would never ever wash off. "So that's how I got my freckles," said Jill with a chuckle. Perhaps Jill's mother was telling the truth about the mischievous elf on her very first Christmas after all?

As the digital clock counted down the days, hours, minutes and seconds to Christmas, the workshop shelves rapidly began to fill up with presents. Aphrodite celebrated by plugging the gramophone into the workshop speakers. When the records played Dylan merrily drummed along to 'Frosty the Snowman,' which Horace loved, and 'Teddy Bear' by someone called *Elvis*, that Teddy and Edward adored.

As for the penguins, they had tremendous fun testing the toys. Prancer took a skateboard for a spin, Blitzen tried on a superhero costume and Dancer played at nine-pin bowling, which was tricky when you only have flippers.

Carol, Edward, Gordon and Nigel went to the games room and tested the latest console games, which were so very different from the old board games at Conjuring Cottage. "They should make one with grumps and a snowball gun, now that would be fun," suggested Nigel.

Meanwhile, Jill was with Jack watching Alf and other elves reading more of the online messages to Santa. "How do they know if the children have been naughty or nice?" asked Jill.

Jack had a smiling face with a halo, "Oh, this is really important. During the year children collect coins in their cart when they're good, but lose them again if they're bad. If they're really naughty they lose all their coins. If a child doesn't get enough coins in a year, then they go on the naughty list."

"But what if they're sorry for being naughty? Doesn't that help them?"

"The elves go on social media to find out what's going on, but they can't send or reply to any messages. Only Aphrodite can decide which children have been far too naughty, and she let's Santa know. If you ask me she's way too generous and forgiving. In my book, there's nothing worse than a very naughty child!" said Jack.

"Jack, really?" said Jill. "That was mean." She went quiet for a bit, played with her fringe then said, "So the elves go on social media? Can I see?"

Aphrodite happened to be close by. She heard what Jill said, "No Jill. It's all strictly confidential. Absolutely no children are allowed to read Santa's messages! They are just for Santa, me and the elves, so absolutely no sneaky or cheeky peaky and for good reason. Christmas can be very painful for some children... it's often why they're naughty and I have to think about all of that before I make my decision... *don't* I Jack?"

Jack nodded and said, "It's against the rules for a player to go online in the workshop."

***

But Jill had a devious plan. When everyone had gone to bed, she sneaked out of the igloo and returned to the elves workshop. She arrived at the front door security key pad, with her robin sat on her shoulder.

"Two, zero, one, two!" she said, entering the numbers into the keypad.

Access Denied. Two Attempts Left.

"I'm sure that was the code?" She tried again with the same numbers.

Access Denied. One Attempt Left.

Jill's robin tweeted in her ear, "Tweet-tweet... tweet-tweet... tweet... tweet-tweet."

"Two, two, one, two. Twenty two, twelve. It's today's date... ah, thank you Paul."

Jill entered the code. The door opened and she went inside. She clicked her fingers and the reception area candles lit up. She carefully took off her boots and tip-toed into the workshop. The digital clock and world map gave her all the light she needed. Far ahead, she was surprised to see a light was on in the elves games room. She reached the desks with the laptops and tablets, and whispered, "What am I doing?"

She sat at a desk, opened a laptop and turned it on. A verse of 'Santa Claus is coming to Town' suddenly started playing and echoed about the workshop. "Shush! Shush!" she cried, flapping her hands at the screen. She waited to check if anyone had heard, but all seemed fine so she looked at the laptop screen.

User Name:

Password:

She fiddled with her fringe and gave this a go, "Mm, User name, Aphrodite. Password, Kat," she said, typing in the letters.

Access Denied

She thought for a bit, then tried, "User name, Aphrodite. Password, Beauty."

The screen changed and read, 'Welcome Aphrodite'. She had hacked the system, "Yes," she whispered in excitement. She opened up the internet then went to her favourite social media site. She entered her mother's name. "Mum!" she whispered. She clicked on the link, looked at the family photos and read through some of the old messages. All her painful memories came flooding back.

Tearfully, she said, "I remember now. There was a fire last Christmas and all was lost, including Jack and Teddy... and our Daddy! *That's* why Edward hates Christmas."

She started to type a message. It read, 'Hi Mum, it's Jill. Edward and I are...'

Suddenly, she heard footsteps coming from the games room and quickly closed the laptop lid to hide the glow of the screen. A boy emerged into the workshop, crossed the floor and stood in front of the world map, looking up at it. Jill could make out his face from the light of the screen. She recognised the turned-up nose and scrawny hair. It was Victor. He started to press buttons on the controllers. It looked like he had one thing on his mind – Sabotage!

"I was happy being a grump. I was happy having the hump. I don't like Christmas, not one bit," he chanted quietly. He clicked his fingers and all the workshop lights came on. Jill could hide no longer. They looked at each other for a few seconds.

"Victor, what are you doing here?" spluttered Jill, wiping away a tear.

"Oh, it's *you*, the Christmas pudding girl. I was in the games room, playing. Why are you here?"

"I heard what you said just now. Why were you pressing those buttons?" asked Jill.

Victor slowly walked towards her, "I heard what you said too. You're not supposed to use the laptops. I was hiding nearby when I heard Aphrodite and the Box Boy tell you it's against the rules. Oh, in case you're wondering... I stowed away on the machine the elves built, that's how I got here. But, hey, just look at you... you're up to no good, aren't you? *Nice!*"

"Shush! This is nothing to do with you," replied Jill.

"You've been blubbering. I suppose you've found out why you're really here, haven't you?" said Victor.

"Why I'm here? It's just a dream and I'll wake up once we finish the game. That's what I know."

"Hmm, you don't get it, do you? This dream picks you for a reason, that's what I know. Well, I don't want to wake up! I like it here and I liked being the General! I see you have one of those annoying robins. I had one once, but I scared mine away," he said with a snigger.

Victor pulled out a chair and sat down next to Jill. Her robin flew off her shoulder and landed on a high shelf. Jill turned off the laptop.

"There... satisfied!" she uttered.

"What do I care? You were going to try to message your parents weren't you? It doesn't matter, Message Delivery Failure! That's what you'd get. I tried to send messages not long after I came here."

"Oh! When was that?" asked Jill.

"Many crappy Christmases ago," he replied.

"*Crappy*? How long is that exactly?" asked Jill.

Victor didn't answer her question. Instead he said, "I've never seen anyone play this game like you two, but... no other players were dumb enough to say they don't believe in Father Christmas three times. Now *that* was stupid. And Edward lost the Santa Sweet, so you're all wasting your time. If it wasn't for that bear he'd still be my Grump King and Christmas would be done for. Oh and another thing, that brother of yours is too old for a teddy. How old is he? He needs to *grow up*."

"If *you* must know, he's eight and I'm ten. Anyway, why do you hate Christmas so much?"

"If *you* must know I hate my parents... I can't do anything right... and they never let me do what I want. They're so strict! Tidy your room... do your homework... blah, blah, blah! And then they told me I've been so bad that I'm getting nothing for Christmas! *Nothing!*" he said.

"I'm sure they didn't really mean it," said Jill.

"I don't care. They totally suck and so does Christmas. I just want it all to stop. Do you get it now? Have I popped your weasel then?"

"Popped my weasel?" replied Jill.

But Victor had decided enough was enough. He ran off. "Victor, wait," cried Jill. But he fled deeper into the workshop and double-clicked his fingers. The lights went out. Jill sat in the near darkness and twiddled her thumbs until her robin flew back. Eventually, she returned to the igloo trying to make sense of all she'd seen and heard.

DOOR TWENTY-THREE

It was Jill's turn to open another of Archie's doors. She did so wondering who exactly was watching her and whether Aphrodite would know she had logged on to a laptop. Behind door twenty-three was a small Christmas tree. She took it out. It was decorated with baubles, fairy lights and tinsel. She showed everyone, but the tree suddenly vanished.

"Most delightful. Outside children!" said Aphrodite, who was again wearing her blonde wig and tiara.

Jill was keen to look at the Christmas tree, but there was something she had to do first. She wondered if the elf-abet blocks could guide her on whether to tell the others she had seen Victor and whether she should try to help him. When the chance came, she knocked them over accidentally on purpose! They tumbled and read, 'F, A, M, I, L, Y' for the second time in their game.

"So that's what you were doing," said Aphrodite, raising her eyebrows.

"I didn't mean to do it," said Jill.

"*Do what*? I'm always knocking the elf-abet blocks over... accidentally, of course... and you just needed a helping hand. Here..." said Aphrodite. She took Jill's hand and led her from the workshop. "Worry not. It's all perfectly marvellous," she whispered.

A wonderful Christmas fir tree had appeared right at the heart of Tinsel Town.

It was as tall as the elves workshop and not too far from it. It was probably the biggest tree in the whole of Santarctica and decorated from top to bottom in baubles, fairy lights and tinsel. Unusually it also had hundreds of white ribbons tied to its branches in heart shapes. The children walked around it, looking up now and again to admire the decorations. The penguins and many of the elves joined them, including Prancer who tipped his head back too far trying, but failing, to see the top. And, you guessed it, he fell onto his bottom *again*!

Carol celebrated the tree by singing, "O Christmas tree, O Christmas tree. How lovely are thy branches."

"They're so unchanging," added Jill. She reached up, and pulled one of the ribbons closer to look at it. All the ribbons had names written on them. "Oh look here, this one says Nigel. And this one says Edward," she said, grabbing another.

"Let me see. So it does," said her brother.

"*Heart*-warming, aren't they? They're the names of every lost child ever to dream this dream. It grows every year to make room for the new ones. I think of them all as my *family*," beamed Aphrodite.

Jill searched the tree for more names. She was after one in particular, reaching up as high as she could on tip-toes to check, but she didn't find the name she was looking for.

"So *every* lost child is here?" she asked.

"Well, almost every one," Aphrodite replied, "A few prove more troublesome than others."

Beside the tree was the big heart-shaped sculpture made from candy canes. It stood upright with a large hole in the middle. The edge of the hole was surrounded by candy cane perches. Robins came and went, landing on the perches for a short while then flying off again.

"And what about the big heart, what's that for?" asked Jill, pointing at the sculpture near the slide.

"Oh, that's the Candy Cane Memory Catcher. When children have *this* dream of Christmas their robins collect the happy memories their parents have of them. Then they fly back to the heart and put those memories inside it. Those happy memories give light to the Christmas Spirit and power Santa's sleigh. It's quite simple really."

"And my robin goes there too?" asked Nigel.

"Yes, Nigel your robin as well. They all do," said Aphrodite.

"What if you're not a real boy?" asked Dylan.

"Yes, what then?" said Horace.

"What about us?" added Teddy.

"Yes Aphrodite, what then?" asked Alf, curiously.

Jack was again sat on Dylan's drum. He had a crying face, "Oh here we go. It's the moment when everyone suddenly feels sorry for the toys."

"Hey, speak for yourself, I'm not a toy," said Alf.

"Oh my darling helpers, without you none of the magic would happen now would it? No toys for any girls or boys! You are the northern lights, the stars in the night sky... and the glow of the moon."

"Far out," said Dylan as he put two fingers up to make the peace sign.

"Right then, I'm glad that's all settled. I'm in the mood for some shortbread and hot chocolate. Who's with me?"

***

But, once everyone had returned to the elves workshop, Jill knew what she had to do. It was her most daring move yet. She grabbed a big handful of shortbread and sneaked off to find her way back to Conjuring Cottage. She passed the Santa Grotto cabin and went into the woods, leaving a trail of shortbread crumbs behind her. She came across wooden signs that read, 'I Wouldn't If I Were You' and 'You Might Be Followed', but the cottage quickly came into view, just as her supply of shortbread ran out.

She ran up to the familiar red front door. The number 6 was still crooked and the 'Please Knock Quietly' sign was still there. She tried the lock. The door opened and she went inside. She dashed up the stairs and ran into Aphrodite's room, ignoring the 'No Children Allowed' sign. She was astonished to find someone sitting on Aphrodite's bed. It was Victor. He was looking through the photograph albums.

"Victor! You made me jump," she cried.

Her robin flew from her shoulder and landed on the shelf weighed down with beauty books.

"What are you doing here? It's against the rules," asked Victor, toying with the AAA medallion about his neck.

"I don't care much about rules. I came here for a reason. I wanted to get something."

"Do you mean the Santa Sweet?"

"No. I've searched everywhere in here for that already. *You* have what I came for. You just beat me to it," she said.

"If you mean the medallion, you can't have it. It's special to me. I'm not letting it go," said Victor, clasping it tightly.

"You can keep it. I came here because of the photo albums... and one of the pictures."

"I remember all these faces," said Victor, looking through an album.

"None of them were like you and Edward. You're different."

"Are we?" she asked, walking over to him. "All these children dreamt of this place for a reason. Maybe it's the same for you," she said.

Jill sat on the bed next to Victor.

"I know why I'm here and I know I'm on the naughty list!" said Victor.

Jill took another album and flicked through the pages until she found Victor's photograph.

"Look, that's you isn't it? You've not changed one bit. Although you've been here for all those Christmases when you wake up just one night will have passed and it'll be Christmas Day. You won't know any different."

"What's the point of that? *My* Christmas has already *been* cancelled!"

"Maybe Aphrodite could help? Just try this?" said Jill. She showed Victor how she twiddled her thumbs.

"Why?" asked Victor.

"Just try it!" said Jill.

Victor twiddled his thumbs. Soon enough, Jill's robin bravely landed on his shoulder and chirped. Victor gave a little smile. Jill touched his hand, and looked more closely at the gleaming medallion. She caught her own reflection in it.

"You should start making happy memories again," said Jill. "You deserve that." She had one eye on the instant camera hanging from the shelf. "Let's start right now. We'll take a selfie... I'll sneak it into Santa's sack. That will get you off the naughty list for sure."

Before Victor could object, she leapt up, grabbed it and took a photo. Click! It slid out from the camera with a strange whirl and slowly began to develop.

"Here. See it's already started, we're making new happy memories."
"Look at me, I'm actually smiling," said Victor, looking at his picture.
"That'll be the Christmas pudding!" joked Jill.

There was a sudden creak on the stairs. The children went quiet. How could Jill possibly explain this to Aphrodite? She gulped. A head popped around the door frame. It was just Kat. Phew! The cat reached up and scratched the frame. The children giggled.

"We better get out of here," said Victor. "I know the way. You can follow me."

"Okay, but I left a shortbread trail just in case I got lost," said Jill.

"Lucky for you I was here. You can't go back to the workshop the way you came. That's Conjuring Cottage for you."

Jill got up and hung the camera back on the shelf. They put the albums back and tidied the bed covers as best as they could.

When they left the cottage it was already beginning to get dark. Thankfully, the Christmas Spirit light burned bright through the treetops. They let it guide them, but had to creep behind a tree when Aphrodite came past on her way home for the night.

"Is that sneaky and cheeky I smell?" she said as she walked by, but didn't stop or turn to look. Jill and Victor watched as Aphrodite flapped her wings and flew the rest of the way to the cottage.

"She really is an angel," said Jill.

But Victor didn't reply.

DOOR TWENTY-FOUR

It was Christmas Eve at last. Archie's final door was waiting to be opened and everyone came together early in Aphrodite's office to cherish the moment. This would be the last of the gifts to add to Archie's list on the office wall. Jill and Edward tugged at the door together. Inside was... NOTHING! The picture on the door gave it away. Behind it was supposed to be the big man with the beard in the red cloak, but Santa Claus had indeed vanished.

"Unimaginable amazeballs! Santa's jingles have gone all jangly," said Aphrodite.

Jack had a frowning face with an open mouth, "Well I'm surprised, *not*! At the risk of stating the obvious, this is all Edward's doing! Congratulations Edward. You win hands down."

"Nonsense Jack!" replied Edward, "We've come too far to give up now. I promised to win this for my father and that's what I'll do."

But the truth was that without the missing Santa Sweet the game was incomplete and there was no opportunity to put right his wrong about not believing in Santa. There were presents galore packed on to the endless shelves, but the workshop was a very gloomy place once more. The Christmas Day countdown clock read 0 days, 15 hours, 45 minutes and 10 seconds. The elves were in the doldrums. They stood about unsure what to do. They just wanted to go through all the gifts on the children's wish lists and load them into Santa's sack. Not only that - the other reindeers were not yet ready and Rudolph's nose still didn't glow.

"Where did I put that sweet?" said Edward, trying his best to remember.

"We're so sticky stuck. We need to unstick the stickiness. If something is lost then it's somewhere it shouldn't be. It's really quite simple," said Teddy. It was a very wise thing to say for a small bear with a head full of fluff, some of which was still poking out from that torn ear.

"Maybe we couldn't find it at the cottage because it wasn't there at all. Maybe someone took it," said Jill.

"But I lost it after door two," said Edward. "The grumps came to the cottage much later than that."

"That's true Edward." Jill was fiddling with her fringe and thinking. She had a suspect in mind.

"Maybe the elf-abet blocks know where the sweet is," said Edward. He picked them up and tumbled them. They read, 'L, I, S, T, -, N.'

"There," said Jack, "I told you right at the start about listening, now didn't I?"

"But it's hard to listen to you when you're such a chatter-box," snapped Edward, "And that's why you have a lid. It's the only way to shut you up sometimes."

Jack snapped back, "No offence Teddy, but Edward is a boy of little brain."

"Watch it Jack or I'll pop your weasel!" said Teddy.

"You lost children and their toys are at it again," said Aphrodite.

“Christmas is a time for goodwill and forgiveness. I said it before and I’ll say it again, ‘things have a habit of turning up when you least expect them too’. Come now, let’s get merry, it's almost Christmas Day. I’m going to put some music on and we’re going to get all those presents loaded into Santa’s sack.”

She did just that, playing the most popular Christmas songs to motivate the elves as they began swiping and packing the presents into Santa’s magical infinitely-big sack. So big in fact that, at times, the elves had to use step-ladders to reach up and put the presents in, but the workshop shelves soon emptied.

All the busyness allowed Jill to creep away unnoticed in search of Victor. She had a good idea where he might be. Jill sneaked out of the workshop, past the Christmas tree, the Candy Cane Memory Catcher, and the Santa Bravo Elite, then made her way up the hill towards Santa's Grotto. There were 52 steps from the bottom to the top, one for every week of the year and a giant slide to come back down again. As Jill climbed the stairs she watched some penguins gleefully whizz down the slide. But she failed to notice an odd group of dodgy-looking elves standing near to Santa's Grotto. When they saw Jill approaching, they hid behind the grotto.

Santa's Grotto was a charming log cabin with a welcoming wooden door and some small windows with shutters on either side. She slowly opened the door and went inside. There was an unlit log fire, a large wooden armchair with a grand red cushion, a spindly table with a pair of round spectacles, an empty mug and china plate, a fluffy white rug and an old chest of drawers with an empty green vase. The mantelpiece over the fire had a pair of candlesticks and a clock just the same as the one at Conjuring Cottage. Above it was an embroidered picture that read, 'Believe in the Magic of Christmas'. A Santa hat and a red hooded cloak with white cuffs and collar was hanging from a coat hook by the door. It had three embroidered letter A's on each of its pockets. Beneath the cloak was a pair of large black clumpy boots.

"Psst, I'm up here," called a voice.

Jill looked up. Victor's head popped out of a small loft hatch. The AAA medallion dangled from his neck. Jill's robin flew through the hatch to explore the loft.

"So that's where you've been hiding," said Jill.

"Is the coast clear? Close the door and I'll come down," he replied.

Victor lowered down a rope ladder, but jumped most of the way to the floor. Neither of them saw the elf spying on them through one of the windows.

"I knew you'd figure it out," said Victor.

"Victor, can I ask you something?"

"You want the Santa Sweet. That's what you were going to ask me, wasn't it? You can't win without it. All those presents will just... go to waste and children the world over will be disappointed." He sat on the large chair and fiddled with his medallion. Jill's robin flew out of the loft and settled on one of the clumpy boots, "Jill, I'm sorry. I..."

Jill rushed over and knelt before him, "You have to help us. You're our only hope."

Suddenly, the Grotto door flew open. In stepped a boy and his teddy. "What is this?" said Teddy. "You're not Father Christmas. Get off his chair," he snapped.

Victor simply replied, "Hello Edward, bear. Have you been naughty or nice this year?"

"That's not funny. Not one bit," fumed Edward.

"Edward... Teddy... this isn't what it seems. I was just..." said Jill.

She stood up and moved away from Victor. Her robin flew to her shoulder.

Edward had interrupted her, "SHUSH! You're my big sister. You're supposed to be looking after me."

"That's just what I'm trying to do."

"How? By sneaking off in the night to the elves workshop to meet *him*? Or by sneaking back to the cottage yesterday to meet *him*? Or by hiding the sweet and pretending that I'd lost it all along. And that's why we followed you," said Edward.

"Edward really, if your father could hear you now," snapped Jill.

"You'd be on the naughty list for sure," said Victor, "No presents for you."

Edward snapped, "Right, General Grump you've had this coming. Let's see what you're really made of shall we?" He shaped his fists and stomped over to Victor.

"That's enough Edward," stormed Jill.

"Oh no it isn't. You're always telling me to be good, but then you tell me lies and feel sorry for the bad guys. It's always the same."

"No, Victor's changed. He wants to wake up and go home, just like all of us."

"She's telling the truth Edward. My days of evil doing are over!" claimed Victor, "And I can prove it. I know where the Santa Sweet is. That's why I came back. It's why I'm sitting in this chair. I want to help you."

"Really, where is it then?" asked Edward.

"I'll show you. Come here Teddy. It's fine I won't hurt you," promised Victor.

"Don't do it Teddy. It could be a trick," said Edward.

But as we know Teddy was the bravest of bear's. He wasn't afraid. He toddled over to Victor.

"Do you remember when we pulled at your good ear?" said Victor.

"Yes! I've got the scars to show for it."

"I'm sorry Teddy. That was when I saw something gold shining in your bad ear. It's why I stopped pulling. I'd planned to pull your ear off completely, even though Edward said what he said. But I just couldn't do it. When I saw what I saw I started to lose my grumpiness. The truth is that you didn't rescue Edward... the magic of Christmas did."

"Are you saying what I think you're saying?" asked Jill, hopefully.

Victor gently put his fingers into the stuffing in Teddy's torn ear and slowly pulled out the Santa Sweet. Pop!

"What a good boy am I?" claimed Victor as he held out the Santa Sweet for all to see.

Edward was so excited, *"It's the Santa Sweet.* It must have fallen into Teddy's ear at breakfast that morning. That's why I couldn't find it. The game is done, we've won. We've won."

"Not quite," said Victor.

He then did something most unexpected. As quick as could be, he unwrapped the sweet, threw the wrapper away, and stuffed it into his mouth before anyone had the chance to stop him.

Victor began to chew furiously. His teeth made a crunching sound as the hard toffee cracked then melted in his mouth.

"What are you doing?" asked Jill.

"It's the only option. I'm doing what must be done," he said with a chuckle. Clutching the AAA medallion, he swallowed the sweet then raised his free hand above his head in victory. Then, with a sparkle and a big red flash, Victor turned into Santa Claus.

Victor tripled in size and had a belly that wobbled like jelly, grew a swirly white beard and a wrinkly jolly face. He grabbed the round spectacles and put them on. His hat, red cloak and boots were waiting by the door.

"Ho, ho, ho, Merry Christmas!" he boomed in a very jolly way.

There was stunned silence, followed by joyful and triumphant cheers that spread all over Tinsel Town and beyond. The elf at the window ducked from view to tell his gang of rebels the news.

"Victor just swallowed the Santa Sweet and turned into the fat old man with the beard."

"Gibberish Oscar, you have to be kidding me."

"Nope."

"I don't believe it!" said a third member of the gang.

"Look for yourself then halfwit."

They all did. They watched Santa get up from his chair, grab his hat and put on his boots and cloak. He strode over to the grotto entrance and gave a big thumbs-up to everyone gathered at the bottom of the hill. The excited penguins saw him and huddled together by the slide. One spun around and slipped on his bottom. It was Prancer, of course.

Led by Alf, many of the elves ran out of the workshop.

"Santa's here! Christmas is saved," yelled Alf.

Santa waved then got on to the slide.

He slid all the way down to the Candy Cane Memory Catcher, laughing loudly as he went. Jill, Edward and Teddy joyfully followed him down the slide. The elves who had spied on them stomped about in bitter disappointment.

"That's it. I'm done with this place. We'll need a new leader," said Oscar.

"I was happy being a grump," said one.

"I was happy having the hump," said another.

"We don't like Christmas, not one bit!" they all mumbled together.

The mood was very different at the bottom of the slide. Santa Claus was quickly surrounded by lots of excited elves, happily leaping and jumping about.

Santa picked some of them up, gave them a hug and put them down again. Aphrodite made her way towards Santa, with Carol, Nigel, Gordon and the others close behind her. At first, Swish flew away because of the cheering, but she quickly returned when she realised why everyone was so happy. She joined the many robins flying about the man in the big red coat. It was quite a sight.

"Miraculously stupendous, we have our Santa back," cried Aphrodite.

Santa strode towards the Candy Cane Memory Catcher. He tapped it firmly, "Good job my chirpy little red-breasted friends. All those happy memories will be just perfect for the reindeer, but first things first. To the workshop there's so much to do."

"How wonderful, Santa's going to get Archie. I just love this bit," said Aphrodite.

Surrounded by his helpers and friends, Santa entered the security code for the workshop.

"Twenty-four, twelve. Christmas Eve! Oh, the very words send shivers down my whiskers!"

The door opened and he went inside. Kat was sat on the reception desk waiting to greet him. "Ahhhh, hello Kat, what a *purr*-fect welcome!" said Santa, tickling a purring Kat behind the ear. It made her tail quiver with joy.

Santa walked into the elves workshop. Kat leapt from the desk and followed him, along with Aphrodite, the children, and everyone else. Teddy's little legs struggled to keep up, so the elves carried him on their shoulders. In the workshop, all the shelves stood empty. Remarkably, every present had already been squeezed into Santa's sack. The countdown clock read, 0 days, 5 hours, 24 minutes and 12 seconds.

In the confusion that followed Santa's sudden arrival, Jack had been left behind on one of the elves desks. He had a 'not amused' face, "'Wait here', they said, so I did. Now look, I've missed all the fun. I was trying to join you all by thinking 'out-of-the-box', which doesn't come easily to me..." But without a further word, Santa came over, picked him up and carried him off towards Aphrodite's office.

"Santa's Clause number eight says, 'When the game is won, piece number one must surely have fun,'" said Santa.

"Hallelujah!" cried Jack.

Santa opened the door to Aphrodite's office. He gave Jack to Jill then walked over to Archie, who was still sitting in the corner, picked him up and carried him off to the workshop. Everyone gathered about him.

"Splendid, now as I said, there's much to do. The magic of Christmas goes way beyond me delivering all those presents to all those children in one night, and squeezing down chimneys and getting through locked doors and windows, sneaking in unseen, eating all those mince pies, and drinking all that milk. Let's begin with Archie, shall we?"

Santa carried Archie over to the countdown clock. Below it was a special hook, above which was a golden plaque with Archie written on it. Santa joyfully hung Archie on the hook and stood back to admire him. He clicked his fingers and the star at the top of Archie shone brightly. The children, the toys and all the elves began to cheer wildly and clap their hands. Dylan celebrated with a glorious drum-roll and Swish swished about triumphantly.

"Right, you're next Jack!" said Santa.

"Ooh, are you going to turn my crank and pop my weasel?" asked Jack.

"Better than that! The elves are going to repair your wonky spring."

Aphrodite burst into song, "From the broken springs on my wing-backed chair. You'll be good as new, most debonair. They'll turn your handle, pop your weasel, the number one jack-in-the box! Yes, the number one jack-in-the-box."

Jack had a kissing face with smiling eyes, "Debonair... which means I'm cool!"

"It's spectacularly wonderfully perfect," said Jill.

Aphrodite giggled.

But Santa had only just begun, "And while they're at it the elves will mend the 'Press Me' button on Rocky's ear, and paint the E's on the elf-abet blocks." A group of elves already had the elf-abet bricks in their hands. Santa took the blocks and rolled them. They fell to the ground and spelt, 'R, -, P, A, I, R.'

"Repair... but what about Teddy?" asked Edward.

Santa agreed. He tapped his nose and said, "Yes, what about him? Where's Edward's Teddy? A Teddy for Eddie? Ed's Ted. Tedward for short?"

"I'm here," said Teddy, with his arm raised, "Is it picnic time for teddy bears?"

Santa laughed, "Ho, ho, not yet, Teddy. Now let's get you fixed up shall we?"

Santa tugged out two of the longest curly hairs from his beard and gave them to Alf, "Here Alf, your talented little elves can use their nimble fingers to stitch-up Teddy's poorly ears."

Edward was delighted, "Imagine it Teddy, a little piece of Santa will forever be part of you."

"Oh goody, goody gumdrops, he can come on all my picnics with me. More tea Santa?"

"Thank you Teddy but milk would do just fine," he replied chuckling.

Sew it was that the elves got busy in the workshop repairing the broken toys. They took one of the sticking-out springs from under Aphrodite's wing-backed chair and used it to replace Jack's wonky spring, stitched Teddy's ears with Santa's whiskers, repainted the E's on the elf-abet blocks, and fixed Rocky's 'Press Me' button.

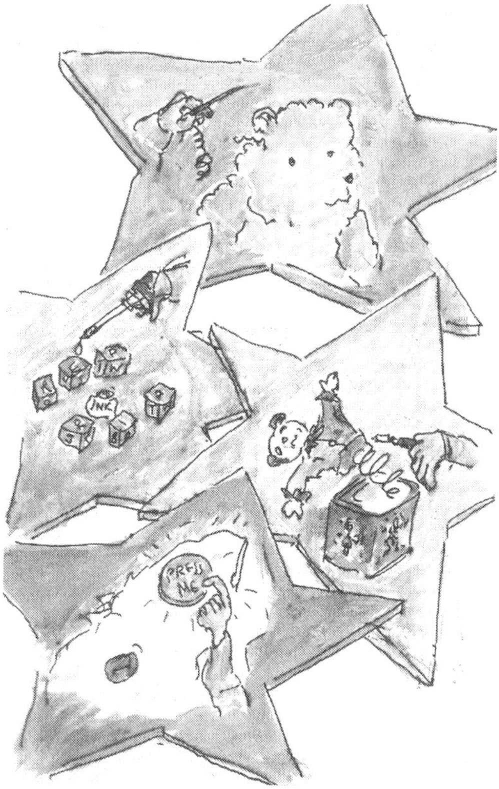

Everybody was thrilled, but poor Nigel's legs still didn't work. Did Santa have anything planned for him? For now, at least, Nigel had the honour of testing Rocky's button for the first time. He pressed it.

"Bethlehem!" said Rocky.

"Wow! That's it, that's the missing word!" cried Carol. She and her singers immediately started singing, "O come all ye faithful, joyful and triumphant. O come ye, O come ye to *Bethlehem*!"

It ended with yet more cheers and a big round of applause from all the elves.

"But what about my legs?" Nigel asked hopefully.

"Yes, what about them?" asked Gordon, "It's my fault they're broken."

"*What*?" asked Nigel.

"I said it's my fault. I didn't catch you."

"But it was an accident. I don't blame you. You tried to save me. You did your best."

Gordon started to cry and hugged his friend.

"I'm so sorry Nigel. Elves can only fix toys, not people," said Alf sadly.

Aphrodite knew what to say, "Fix or no fix, let's get one thing perfectly clear! Nigel... you're differently-abled, but equally valued. And you certainly showed those grumps whose boss!"

"I did, didn't I? Got them good and proper!" he said, miming out how he aced that snowball machine.

***

The elves may have repaired the broken gifts, but the truth was the grumps were never truly beaten. Grown-ups would always grumble about Christmas. So, Bah Humbug would rise from its ruins and the grumps would choose a new general and seek a king. The bad elves skulking near Santa's Grotto would be the first of next year's grumps, but they hadn't quite given up on this year yet!

"We can still stop Christmas. The fat man's sleigh can't fly without the reindeers," said Oscar.

"We could kidnap them," said another.

"But we don't know where they are."

"*Crikey*, how long have you guys worked here?" asked Oscar.

"Too long Oscar. I'm so sick of Santa, tinsel and presents," replied another elf.

"We just need to grab the penguins," said Oscar.

"*The penguins*?"

"Yes the penguins... the little black and white birds with flippers that waddle about," said Oscar sarcastically.

"I know what a penguin looks like."

"But Oscar they don't look like reindeer and they can't fly."

"Just trust me. Look they're coming back up the steps to have another go on the slide. Let's grab them and lock them in the grotto. That should do it."

***

Back in the elves workshop, the Christmas countdown continued. The clock read, 0 Days, 3 hours, 10 minutes.

Santa asked, "We've checked the list?"

Alf replied, "Twice."

"And we know who's been naughty or nice?"

"We do."

"Then it's time for me to get the sack!" said Santa.

"It's ready for you," said Alf, "Every present for every child is in it."

Edward had another brilliant question, "But shouldn't you read the letters to Santa? We all wrote to you."

"They did indeed Edward. Worry not, their every word is in my heart. It's all part of the magic of Christmas."

Santa picked up the sack and threw it over his shoulder, "Heave, hi, ho. It's off to work I go."

"Wait," cried Jill, "You've dropped one... here," she said, quickly tucking something deep into the sack.

"Why thank you young lady," he said with a knowing wink. "To the sleigh!" he called.

Santa carried the sack out of the workshop, with the children following close behind. Edward held Teddy's paw and Jill carried Jack, who was happily bouncing about in his box on his shiny new spring. Carol had a feeling that the elf-abet blocks would be needed, so she brought them. The route to the Santa Bravo Elite was lined with crowds of ecstatic elves, whooping, cheering and chanting, "Santa! Santa! Santa!" The big man smiled broadly and waved to the crowd. He reached the sleigh and heave-hoed the heavy sack on to the back.

"It's the latest model," said Alf, "It flies like a dream. We already have Rudolph. We just need to rein-up the rest of the reindeer."

"Ah Rudolph, but there's a problem with his nose, we'll have to put that right. Now where are my little flipper friends, Dasher, Blitzen, Cupid?" called Santa.

"They're already on their way back up to the Grotto," said Alf.

"Oh I simply adore this bit," said Aphrodite.

As the penguins hopped up the stairs, the elves moved the Candy Cane Memory Catcher in front of the slide, so that the hole in the middle lined up perfectly with the end of the slide. All eight penguins had gathered at the Grotto.

"Dylan, a drum roll if you please," requested Aphrodite.

Dylan did just that, but the gang of grumpy elves decided it was time for action.

"Now, get them," ordered Oscar.

"But they're slippery and smell like fish."

"Yeah, and those flippers look real mean."

"We're out numbered Oscar."

"Do I have to do everything myself? They're only penguins. How hard can it be?"

Oscar had eight penguins to choose from. He tried to grab hold of Dasher.

"*Excuse me*?" said Dasher.

"You're coming with me," demanded Oscar.

But Dasher spun around fast and whacked Oscar with his flipper, "*Oi*, I've waited all year for this. I'm going to fly!" he said.

Oscar took a tumble and lost his hat. He went scrambling after it. "That didn't go to plan. I'm off to Bah Humbug. Who's with me?" cried Oscar.

Dasher hopped on the slide head first. He slid on his belly all the way down and through the hole in the Candy Cane Memory Catcher. *Whoosh!* He transformed into a majestic reindeer, landing on all four hooves then doing a little leap of joy.

The other penguins quickly followed, one by one - Dancer, Prancer, Vixen, Comet, Cupid, Donner and Blitzen. They each transformed into magnificent reindeers, glistening with the spirit of Christmas.

"*Wow*... that was so amazing," said Carol, as the other reindeers greeted Rudolph.

"Wasn't it just? It brings tears to my eyes. And look now, do you see Rudolph's nose, how it glows!" replied Aphrodite.

"It surely does, it glows," said Jill.

Santa was delighted, "Now with his nose so bright, he can drive my sleigh tonight."

"Rein them up," said Alf. He pointed his bony finger at each reindeer in turn, "Dasher, Dancer, Prancer, Vixen, Comet, Cupid, Donner, Blitzen and... Rudolf!"

The reindeer lined up two-by-two with Rudolph leading the way. The elves reined up the reindeer and decorated them with jingle bells. Santa was all set.

"That's odd," said Jill, "I always thought Santa's sleigh had eight reindeer, but there are nine!"

"This year's extra special. Rudolph earned his place at the front for bringing you here in time... without his help Christmas would have been cancelled," said Aphrodite.

Santa puffed out his rosy cheeks and climbed aboard his sleigh. The joyful children and elves huddled about it, as the reindeer snorted, stamped their hooves and swished their tails. Ahead of them the runway was lit by two rows of flashing fairy lights.

Santa gave one last wave to the crowd, "Joy to the world. Ho, ho, ho, I've got to go! Dash on Rudolph, dash on Dasher." The reindeer broke into a trot, which became a canter, then a gallop, as the sleigh raced down the runway picking up speed. In a glorious swish and whoosh the sleigh gracefully took off and headed upwards. Far below, the children cheered as all the elves threw their hats into the air and Horace doffed his top hat as high as his stick arms would allow. Carol, Nigel and Gordon sang, "Santa Claus is coming to town, Santa Claus is coming to town!"

"Ho, ho, ho, Merry Christmas everybody! Merry Christmas!" cried Santa. His words echoed all over Santarctica and began the celebrations across the world. The Santa Bravo Elite looked spectacular against a starry night sky as it circled above Tinsel Town.

Teddy was watching the sleigh, "Round and round goes Santa like a teddy bear? One stop, two stops, his presents go everywhere."

Edward rejoiced, "*I love Christmas!* I really love it."

"*Do you Edward?*" asked Jill, "I didn't want to tell you, but I've remembered what happened to our family last Christmas. You've been so brave. Daddy would be so proud. You grew up fast Edward and with Teddy's help." She kissed her brother's cheek, accidentally bumping into Carol and causing the elf-abet blocks to tumble from her hands. They read, 'S, A, V, I, O, R.'

"Savior?" asked Edward.

"Salvation for the lost children plucked like magic from thin air. It's what you both wanted from the very beginning, remember?" said Aphrodite, as she shed a single tear of joy. It dropped from her cheek, was caught by a sharp gust of wind, lifted up and struck Santa's circling sleigh. Aphrodite's tear sparkled like a diamond in the sky.

"That's one extra wish with Swish!" said Swish, not that any of the children heard.

"That's outta sight man!" said Dylan.

The Santa Bravo Elite soared away into the night. It flew over the heads of bucking unicorns, the Candy Cane Forest and two polar bears standing and waving Santa on his way. Santa spotted them and gave them a hearty wave as the sleigh sped off.

***

As a reward for all their hard work the elves had fun in the Tinsel Town fairground. The children and the toys joined in, taking turns on the rocking horse carousel, hair-raising roller-coaster and dodgem cars.

Carol, Nigel and Gordon sang some of their favourite Christmas carols and songs. It was fab for Dylan as he got his wish of being in a band by playing along to some of the songs. Alf, too, got to play his air-guitar and with a real guitar at that!

While they all celebrated, Oscar and his grumpy gang of elves made their way to the Whatchamacallit, climbed aboard, started the engines and headed back to Bah Humbug.

"Isn't this stealing?" said one of the gang.

"Of course it's stealing stupid. Mark my words, the grumps will be back next year," warned Oscar.

"Uglier, grumpier and meaner than ever," agreed another, as the bumbling-bee of a craft left Tinsel Town behind.

***

Aphrodite had spotted the Whatchamacallit as it buzzed-off from Tinsel Town, but it troubled her not because she knew when children dreamed this dream of Christmas it was a never-ending struggle of good versus bad! Besides, Aphrodite was overjoyed because a new name had been added to the ribbons on the Christmas tree. That name was *Victor*.

"*Kat*-astrophy avoided," she told Kat, who purred loudly, just as Jill and Edward sneaked up on them both. Edward whispered something into his sister's ear and they giggled.

"Whispering, sneaky! Giggling, cheeky!" said Aphrodite. "I've stupendous news. Look children, do you see Victor's name is on the tree."

"But I'm worried. What will become of him?" asked Jill.

"Yes, will Victor be Santa forever now?" added Edward.

"Oh no children, he'll simply stay in the dream as Father Christmas until players who have this dream say... and they *will* say it... that thing they absolutely shouldn't say three times in their game. When that happens Santa will disappear and Victor's dream will be over!" she said smiling.

"But what happens in that game if someone bites the head off the Santa Sweet first?" Edward dared to ask.

Aphrodite shuddered, "Dear child should such a ghastly thing happen... and it can... then that's an entirely different matter altogether... and a story for another day."

"Good job you didn't do that then Edward!" said Jill smugly.

"Now, now!" said Aphrodite. "For all is joyful and triumphant. Victor lived up to his name, didn't he? What a winner! He was the grump that saved Christmas."

***

And save Christmas Victor did. Santa and his reindeer visited every child across the world in just a single night. Quite how they did it nobody really knows, perhaps it was the never-ending supply of mince pies, milk and carrots that kept them going.

And this year, Santa left every child a clementine orange as a reminder to their parents not to grumble too much about Christmas.

There was one house that Santa looked forward to visiting the most. It was the one where Jill and Edward lived. There was nothing special about their house. It was just an ordinary home, in an ordinary street, in an ordinary town, but it meant the world to him. He slipped down the chimney, crept into their rooms and caught them sleeping. It was a strange thing indeed for he knew what they were dreaming. Santa gleefully left them both a special present in a stocking at the end of their beds. Then he went to the lounge and put their other gifts under the tree. A happy elf on the shelf had been waiting for him and joyfully popped into his sack, before Santa returned to his sleigh to carry on with his work. "Geronimo," cried the elf.

DOOR TWENTY-FIVE

On Christmas Day in Tinsel Town, Edward woke everyone early with the loudest snore he'd ever done. The children sprang from their beds, but were surprised to find they were still in the igloo and *the dream*. They quickly got dressed and dashed to the elves workshop. It was eerily quiet for all but one of the elves was sleeping-off the night before. The world map bleeped as it tracked Santa's movements. The screen showed that the Santa Bravo Elite was flying over Canada and it wasn't dawn there yet, so his work for the night wasn't done.

Aphrodite had been waiting for the children in her office, wearing her glamorous blond wig, white gown and tiara, "Merry Christmas, my precious little darlings! I'm afraid to say its way past waking up time. Oh and I do apologise for my clown face. I promised myself I wouldn't cry, but these are tears of joy, not sadness."

Teddy, Jack, Dylan, Rocky, Horace and Swish watched as Aphrodite hugged each child in turn.

"Thank you so much Aphrodite... for helping us... all of us," said Jill.

"You really are an angel," added Edward.

"Beautiful on the inside and the outside," insisted Carol.

"We've had the time of our lives," said Nigel.

"We'll never forget you," cried Gordon.

Aphrodite replied, "But the real magic is that you saved yourselves children."

"We're a little sad though," said Edward, "I just wish we could have helped Nigel to walk again."

Swish reminded Edward, "Two wish Swish. Swish wish two." But her voice was so quiet that nobody heard her – *again!* Not even Nigel, "It's okay. At least I got to ride on Rocky, which was a dream come true," he said, fondly patting Rocky on the neck.

"That's the stuff kiddo, chin up," said Alf, tapping under his own chin.

"And as for you Buddy," he told Edward, "Come here!" Edward did so.

As they hugged, he said, "Goodbye Alf. I'm really going to miss you."

"Ah, cut it out," replied Alf, "I'll be at your house next Christmas, just you see. Alfie the Elfie sitting on your shelfie."

"Cheers Buddy!" replied Edward.

Aphrodite twiddled her thumbs. The children's robins came over to her, "Now my little darlings fly away home. Go catch those happy Christmas memories."

The robins flew from view. Aphrodite opened door number 25 in her office - the one with the 'No Toys Allowed' sign.

"Come children, it's time to go. This way, but alas, no toys," she said.

"What, not even Teddy?" Edward asked.

"I'm sorry Edward. It's the rules."

"So Jack can't go either?" asked Jill.

"The pieces must stay behind. It's not their dream, so they don't need to wake up. Only the children do."

"But I'll never see Teddy again... and the elf-abet blocks said that Carol, Nigel and Gordon were pieces, so why are they allowed to leave, when Teddy can't? *It's not fair*!" said Edward.

Jack popped up from his box to seal his own fate, "Santa's clause number nine is to blame. When children enter this dream of Christmas as pieces through Archie's door six then the 'No Toys Allowed' rule doesn't apply. It's just the way things are!"

"That's a stupid rule!" snapped Edward, tearfully.

"Now be brave," said Teddy. "You always wanted to grow up and now's your chance. I'll be deep in your heart if you need me. We're sticky stuck forever. Edward's Ted, a teddy for Eddie. Tedward for short." Edward gave Teddy the tightest hug ever and counted all the way to twenty-five before letting go. He hugged the other toys too, but not Jack. He just winked at him. Jack had a winking face too, "Bye little winker!" he said.

"Oh Jack. Can I turn your crank once more?" asked Jill.

"The pleasure is all mine," he said. Jill did so and Jack popped his weasel. He had a grinning face with big eyes, "And don't worry Jill. Rules are rules. I'm not one to break them."

"But I am," she said, fiddling with her fringe.

Aphrodite put an end to that idea, "Not this time. Absolutely no sneaky cheeky! It's just a precaution. I'm sorry."

Edward and Jill felt a little lost without their toys, so Aphrodite sang a special song for them,

"When children dream of Christmas, I hope they dream of me,
of someone so spectacular, Aphro-di-te!
When children dream of Christmas, I hope it's full of joy,
Santa and adventure and all their favourite toys.
That it's marvellous, stupendous, fabulous and cool.
When children dream of Christmas, I hope their dreams come true!"

Kat flapped her ears and meowed.

"Follow me children, it's Christmas Day. It's time for you all to wake up," she said as she flew through door number 25. Edward, Jill, and Carol followed, while Nigel was back in his wheelchair with Gordon pushing him. Aphrodite closed the final door in the dream and led the children up a long corridor, which became brighter and brighter with every step. Ahead the spirit of Christmas shone gloriously. It was so bright that Aphrodite had put on her sunglasses to keep her in the dream. As the children moved ever closer to the light they suddenly felt themselves being lifted up by its magical power.

They heard Aphrodite's voice grow ever fainter, "Merry Christmas children. I love you all."

The children's dream of Christmas was over.

CHRISTMAS MORNING

When children dream of Christmas then wake up on Christmas morning it's a rare and special thing. Edward was in that strange place between sleep, dreams and wakefulness. For a moment, he could almost see Aphrodite standing in his room at the end of his bed smiling.

Edward had been on a wonderful adventure which would change him forever. He rubbed the sleep from his eyes and felt for his teddy. Then he remembered, Teddy was *lost* in the fire at their old house last Christmas, and this would be the first Christmas without his father around. But as painful as this was, because of the dream Edward was full of the Christmas Spirit and his heart glowed.

His bedroom was most ordinary with simple furniture, superhero figures and toy models. At the end of his bed was a Christmas stocking. He scrambled out from under the covers to look inside. He pulled out a clementine and laughed. Hidden among the other small gifts was a gold medallion with the letters AAA engraved on it.

"A, A, A for Archie's Advent Adventure? This was General Grump's key. Oh my, I have to show Jill," he said to himself.

He quickly put the medallion around his neck.

Edward threw on his dressing gown and slippers and dashed to his sister's room. She was already downstairs in the lounge, so Edward ran down to join her.

"Edward, there you are sleepy head. I was just coming to wake you," said his mother, standing in the doorway to the lounge. She had her hair in a pony tail and was wearing a red dressing gown and new reindeer-faced slippers.

"I just needed my forty winks," joked Edward. He started winking, left eye then right.

"Your forty winks?" chuckled his mother, "You are funny Edward. Well it worked, those dark circles under your eyes have disappeared at last... and look Santa's been, he ate the mince pie and drunk some of the milk." She kissed Edward on the top of his head, and ruffled his hair, "Happy Christmas son," she said, trying her best not to cry.

"And the reindeer ate the carrot," said Jill.

Edward walked into the lounge. He took a long look at their Christmas tree, especially at the angel sitting on the top. It reminded him of Aphrodite. The tree also had a Christmas fairy, jingle bells and decorative crackers just like the one he'd pulled with Carol at Conjuring Cottage, and fake clip-on candles with little labels. Edward clicked his fingers to see if they would come on, but they didn't.

"Edward, you clicked your fingers! Well I never," said his mother.

"I've been practising!"

"And what's that around your neck?" his mother asked.

"Oh, I found it in my Christmas stocking. Santa left it for me. Look, it says A, A, A."

"A, A, A, that's strange," said Jill, "I dreamt about that medal last night."

"You dreamt about Archie's Advent Adventure?" asked Edward.

"I did."

"Wow, that's so weird," replied Edward.

"... and ridiculous," she added.

"Edward are you sure you're okay?" asked his mother.

"Don't worry mummy, I'm fine. Let's open our presents," said Edward.

"Yes, let's Edward," said Jill.

"Oh children I'm so relieved. I've been terribly worried because of what happened last year. I still want today to be special somehow. It's what your father would want to."

Their mother gazed out of the lounge window. A light snow was falling and a pair of robins had settled on the window ledge. Jill and Edward noticed them. They left their presents unopened and scampered to the window. Edward and Jill looked at each other knowingly and began to twiddle their thumbs, causing the robins to hop about excitedly.

"Come back Peter... come back Paul," they sang, as their mother shook her head.

On the lawn was a snowman with a top hat, carrot for a nose, pebbles for eyes and sticks for arms.

"It's Horace," said Jill.

"But not Horrid," replied Edward.

The children looked at each other in amazement and giggled.

"What's so funny?" asked Mother, "Oh, there's a snowman in the yard. How did that get there? And look there's a pair of robins sitting on his hat."

"Santa must have made it," joked Edward.

"Do you know children that some people say that robins collect all the happy memories?"
"Yes, we know that mummy," replied Jill, "Come on, let's open the presents now."

The robins flew back to the window ledge and watched as the children began to unwrap their presents. There were the things you might expect for children of their age like digital consoles and games. But to their mother's surprise, Edward and Jill just put them to one side. They were hoping for other presents and weren't disappointed.

The first special gift was addressed to them both and signed, 'love Alf'. They opened it together. Six wooden blocks fell to the floor. The elf-abet blocks spelt, 'P, R, I, Z, E, S'.
"Prizes?" asked Mother.
"The elf-abet blocks never lie. Let's open another one," urged Edward.

Two of their presents looked just the same. They opened these next.
"It's my Christmas jumper," said Edward.
"So is mine! Ooh, it has the Christmas pudding on it," Jill said, lifting it up to show her brother.
"And mine's got a teddy on it!"
Surprised, their mother shook her head again.

Jill opened another gift. It was pretty obvious what was inside because of its shape.
"Look Edward, it's a rocking horse! He's white and all bridled up. He has a glorious mane, buttons for eyes, a swishy tail and a 'Press Me' button."
"Rocky? It's Rocky," cried Edward.
Mother was puzzled, "Well, I don't know... that's a surprise."
"Press the button. Does it work?" asked Edward.
Jill sat on the horse and pressed the button.
Rocky said, "Bethlehem! Bethlehem!"
The children giggled, but their mother didn't get the joke, not one bit.

Edward opened another present. Inside was a drum held by a wooden boy with a large furry hat, scarlet jacket and white trousers. The drummer boy had a wind-up key on his back.

"It's Dylan. It's really Dylan," said Edward.

"That's outta sight Man!" replied Jill. Edward giggled.

"A drummer boy called *Dylan*?" asked their mother with a very confused face.

"Wind him up. See what he plays," urged Jill.

Edward did so. The children knew the tune and the song played by the clockwork drummer. They sang, "Come they told me, pa rum pa pa rum. A new born king to see pa rum pa pa rum. Our finest gifts we bring, pa rum pa pa rum. To lay before the king, pa rum pa pa rum."

"What in the name of Christmas is happening?" asked Mother.

Jill grabbed her last gift. She was really hopeful because the present was just the right shape and size. She ripped the wrapping paper off.

"Jack. *Is it you*? Is it really you?" she cried excitedly.

It was a jack-in-the-box for sure with juggling jester figures on the outside. She looked underneath. *Jill* was written on the bottom. She turned the crank handle and the music played.

Edward and Jill sang along, "Half a pound of tuppeny rice, half a pound of treacle. That's the way the money goes. Pop..." Up came Jack. He had a smiling face, "Goes the Weasel!"

"Let me see that," asked Mother. "This is *impossible*. Pinch me I must be dreaming. Jack was destroyed in the fire last Christmas, but it's the same one. We got this for your First Christmas... and the spring has been repaired... how wonderful," she said tearfully.

Edward grabbed his last present and tore the paper off so fast he almost tore an ear on his beloved Teddy.

"*Teddy! It's you!* My Teddy, you came back. Santa made it happen."

"This is *too* much. That's Tedward. We lost him in the fire too," said Mother.

Edward hugged his bear tightly and his mother cried tears of joy. "Look, his ear is all stitched up with white thread... but I don't understand. You're father went back into the house to try to rescue these after he saved you... and then... and," she said sobbing.

Naturally, her children rushed over and hugged her tightly.

"Let's go take Teddy and Jack to see your father," said Mother, once she'd stopped crying.

"We were thinking that too, weren't we Edward."

"Yes Jill, we were."

"Let's wear our Christmas jumpers," said Jill. Edward nodded.

***

Father was in a very deep sleep. He'd been that way for a whole year since the dreadful fire that almost took everything they owned. He was in a hospital wired up to machines and was drip-fed by tubes that gave him enough energy and goodness to keep him going. The doctors said he was very lucky to be alive and that the amount of smoke he breathed in had sent him into a deep sleep. They said his brain was resting. It was called a coma. They didn't know if he would ever wake up again. If he did they didn't know if he would even remember who he was anymore.

The children visited their father often. They spoke to him, played him music, read him stories, held his hand and told him how much they loved and missed him. For this Christmas, the first anniversary of the fire, they had made their own paper-chain and snowflake decorations and put them up in their father's hospital room. Now, on Christmas Day, they arrived to see him again.

Mother walked in wearing sunglasses, a brown shaggy coat and clumpy boots. Her hair was no longer in a ponytail and all messed up as it had been blown about by the wind on the way to the hospital.

Mother took off her coat and hung it up on a hook by the door. "Merry Christmas darling," she said to her husband, "The children are here. We've had quite a morning." She took off her sunglasses, worn to hide her red tearful eyes.

Edward had Teddy in his arms and the AAA medallion around his neck. Jill was holding her jack-in-the-box. They went over to their father's bed.

"Merry Christmas Daddy," said Jill brightly. She kissed her father's cheek and stood next to him, "We've had a really *amazing* morning, haven't we Edward?"

"Yes... hello Daddy, Happy Christmas," said Edward, quietly. He had so much he wanted to say, but didn't really know where to begin. He sat down on a cold plastic chair close to the bed and put Teddy on his lap. He put one hand on the AAA medallion and looked at all the tubes and the medical machines. He felt all the Christmas joy start to slip away.

Jill gently tapped the back of his head, "What's up Kat got your tongue?" she asked. Edward smiled a fake smile. "Tell Daddy about the bear," said Jill.

"Okay!" he replied.

Edward got to his feet and lifted Teddy up so his father could see him. "Look what Santa brought me last night," he said. He waited, hoping for a reply that sadly didn't come, "It's Teddy and his ear is all fixed... good and proper. He's been such a brave little bear. Nothing scares him, not even the grumps. He went right into Bah Humbug to rescue me."

Jill interrupted him, ".... with his polar bear friends but General Grump trapped them so we had to go rescue him, didn't we Edward?"

Edward's face lit up. "We did! And the General had this medallion... it's a key," he said, removing the medal from around his neck. He put the medallion in his daddy's hand and closed his fingers around it.

Jill continued, "And Jack had a wonky spring and a hundred different faces to match his mood." She showed the jack-in-the-box to her father. "When we were at Conjuring Cottage he told us the rules to Archie's Advent Adventure... he said it was *really* important to listen carefully... that we had to open all the doors on the right days... and... well Jack kept getting things mixed up because of his spring, but the elves fixed him with one of the springs from Aphrodite's big chair."

Edward went on, "Aphrodite's a Christmas Angel. She was weird, but really kind. Beautiful on the inside... and outside... and the elves fixed Teddy's ear with a whisker from Santa's beard."

Jill interrupted again, "And Jack pops up perfectly now Daddy, *listen,*" she said and turned the crank handle. Jill and Edward sang along to the tune, "Half a pound of tuppeny rice, half a pound of treacle, that's the way the money goes, pop!" And Jack popped up.

"*Goes the weasel,*" sang their father. He had opened his eyes for the first time in a year and said his first words for just as long.

"DADDY!" screamed Edward and Jill, "You're awake!"
Their mother cried out with joy, "*Victor*! Victor! My Victor."
"This is the best *ever* day in the world by far... ever, ever, forever!" said Jill joyfully.

"Clare, Jill, Edward... and Teddy and Jack," he said looking about.
"Where am I? I had the most amazing dream about Christmas. It seemed to go on for years. How long have I been asleep?"
"Let's not worry about that now... it's Christmas Day darling!" said Clare.

A nurse had dashed into the room having heard all the excitement. She was a tall woman with long blonde hair, called Angela, who had helped care for Victor all these months. She was holding something in her hand. It was a small gift with a strange label 'Victor, Room 6, Ward 25, The Hospital, England.'
"You're awake. It's a miracle. How absolutely marvellously stupendous," she said joyfully, "And on Christmas Day too."

Victor shuffled up in his bed, "Oooh, I'm stiff," he said, sitting up and tightly gripping the medallion in his hand, "Now children, let me get a good look at you. My you've grown. And look Edward you still have Teddy, I thought..."

Edward interrupted him, "I know, you said I was too old for Teddy and..."

But his father held up his hand to stop him. He tapped his nose and said, "Eddie's Teddy. Ed's Ted. A Teddy for Edward. Tedward for short. Oh Edward, I'm sorry for what I said. You can keep that bear for as long as you wish. You grow up when you're good and ready. I guess I just had a bad case of the Christmas grumps when I said it."

As the children giggled, Victor put the medallion over his head.

The nurse smiled knowingly and said, "I believe this is for you?" She passed the gift to Victor, "I'll be back with some hot chocolate and scrumptious shortbread... oh, and some doctors."

Victor's hands trembled as he opened the gift, "What is this? A photograph? Wait a second. This is from one of those old instant cameras. Jill, it's you... and a boy. He looks just like me when I was about your age. There's a robin on his shoulder... and he's wearing this medallion around his neck."

Clare asked, "Victor, let me see that. I've never seen a picture of you as a child, not since..."

"Me neither, not for a long while. It's all coming back to me though. It was many years ago before I was adopted. I just had the same dream again. It's how I knew the fire would happen when it did. It's why I rushed home and saved you all from the flames, but I couldn't save the toys and now they're back."

The astonished children looked at each other. It seemed that through the magic of Christmas their father had somehow been Santa Claus this year. *Could it really be so*? Indeed their father seemed to know what they were thinking. "Ho, ho, ho. Merry Christmas!" he said in a deep and jolly voice.

At which point the nurse returned with the hot chocolate and shortbread for everyone. She announced, "Oh, we've some carol singers in the ward today raising money for the local orphanage. It would be simply perfect if they could sing for you, shall I wave them in?"

But it was too late. Three singers had already gathered behind her in fancy dress. There were two boys and a girl. The girl was wearing a long crimson dress and had a gold paper crown on her head. Her hair was red with ringlets and she had beautiful eyes with big eyelashes. "Hello, Merry Christmas... I'm Carol, this is Gordon and that's Nigel," she said.

Gordon was thinner than he was in the dream and Nigel... well Nigel... was walking again. Swish, it seemed, had granted Edward's wish.

Oh, and, "tweet, tweet-tweet, tweet-tweet-tweet," for three robins had flown into the ward with the singers, which meant only one thing. Like Gordon and Nigel, Carol, too, had found her forever home.

The children's dream of Christmas had indeed been far stranger than they could ever have imagined. In celebration, Carol and her singers sung, and the children, their parents and the nurse joined in,

"O come all ye faithful, joyful and triumphant.
O come ye, O come ye to Bethlehem.
Come and behold him, born the king of angels.
Oh come let us adore him, O come let us adore him, O come let us adore him, *Christ the Lord*!"

- The End -

A WORD FROM THE AUTHOR

Edward And The Christmas Grumps was crafted in a fury of activity around Christmas 2017. I tinkered with the story in autumn 2018, adding watercolour illustrations and an animated video featuring the Grump Grumble. Follow on Facebook @ChristmasGrumps

My debut novel 'The Earth Emperor's Eye' issued in 2015. In 2017, I adapted it into a seven-part screenplay. I'm currently reworking the style and content to better fit with the screenplay, and aim to republish the story in Spring 2019.

Both stories celebrate the real magic of Christmas. They also have a spiritual connexion because I sense something beyond, a guiding light. I also cherish the beauty of life on Earth. It's all perfectly wonderful and a terrible travesty and legacy of this generation to destroy such a majestic miraculous blessing.

Joy to the World!

Printed in Great
Britain
by Amazon

31679617R00174